James Freil was born in 1958 and at UCNW, Bangor. He wo Wales. His first novel, *Left of k......, won a Betty Trask* Award.

Also by James Friel in Abacus:

TAKING THE VEIL

JAMES FRIEL

Left of North

An Abacus Book

First published in Great Britain by Macmillan London Limited, 1987
Published in Abacus by Sphere Books Ltd, 1991

ISBN 0 349 10201 5

Printed and bound in Great Britain by
BPCC Hazell Books
Aylesbury, Bucks, England
Member of BPCC Ltd.

Sphere Books Ltd
A Division of
Macdonald & Co (Publishers) Ltd
165 Great Dover Street
London SE1 4YA

A member of Maxwell Macmillan Publishing Corporation

Contents

Part One **North**

Part Two **Left**

Part Three **Left of North**

Part One

NORTH

Chapter One

A Hole Somewhere North

This story began in the North, in a place called Little Atherton, but it did not end there as perhaps it should have done. It's difficult to say whether it did end or whether, as seems more likely, it simply continued. It probably continued. It probably went on for years, blindly, without rest or interruption, but if it ever did end then it ended somewhere well to the left of North.

Little Atherton was a dismal, wet-Sunday of a place, built on the slant of a slight and undramatic valley. Looked at from above – where it looked no better than it did from the streets – the view was mostly of semi-corrugated houses and crescent-shaped tower blocks, smoky grey with wooden curtains nailed over broken windows. Standing out from behind the dullish red swoop of council houses that spread throughout the town were the blackened walls of mills and warehouses, six in all, each empty and, those that still had roofs, grass-thatched from age and disuse.

To the right of the town were five generous acres of balding park. The park, surrounded by shabby, anorexic trees, boasted three swings, two broken, one roundabout, vandalised, and one cracked tarmac tennis court.

To the far left of the town, and under one domed roof, lay its two-storeyed shopping centre, police station, library and clinic. The complex and all that it contained was turned in upon itself, only its globed and graffiti-sprayed walls on show. The shops inside this grubby oyster had mostly nothing on show other than TO'I'LET fingered in the whitewash that covered their windows and only the clinic could claim a crowd. At night the sign that ran around its curved walls in capital letters of red neon glowed weakly in the dark:

T_E H_RR_ _YAM_ ARNDAL_ CENTR_
CAR PARK
__LICE __BRA__ ___NIC.

A strong wind blew in Little Atherton and the vandals were quite athletic. The missing letters were never replaced. It was too costly. The sign stayed as it was, like an unfinished game of hangman.

Beyond and around Little Atherton lay other towns, packed so closely together that only a native knew where

2

one town ended and another began. There was Roston, Mallet, Humsey, Petergate and other shabby new towns with litter round their feet, all alike, all merging into one vast, rusted-steel and cement park. Only its name, its award-winning complex and the Rucks distinguished Little Atherton from its neighbours. The name was no poem and the complex just a joke, but the Rucks, now they were special.

The Rucks were two monstrously tall and sloping slackheaps. Mountainous and black-faced, they stood side by side in the almost exact centre of the town, identical in shape, colour and size, mirror images. They reared up and shadowed the whole town like a tidal wave about to smash down upon it. It was useless to describe Little Atherton without describing the Rucks, impossible to think of the place without seeing them in your mind.

The Rucks looked as if they had always been there, natural landmarks, but, like the town, they had grown up around the now-deserted railway yard. Trains carrying slack from the Overton Collieries used to be repaired and stored in the yard. In its day the yard had covered acres and had provided Little Atherton with most of its work. Now the yard was just one more area of waste land. There was nothing left of it but the charred ribs of its burnt-out warehouses. The scars left by the tracks had been healed over and the railway was now a grassy walkway, a short cut to the school, and, in summer, a bright feast of purple weeds.

Little Atherton was a dying town, but while other towns could claim that they too were in a state of decay and that they too had their problems no other town had the Rucks with which to deal. Not only did they remind the town of the work and the wealth it had once enjoyed,

3

the former prosperity of which they were the grim mementoes, but they also disfigured it and made a plain town ugly. What future was there for a town with two such residents? If the good times were ever to pass by again how could the town ever tempt them to stay? Those black-faced giants would frighten off the bravest good fairy.

The Rucks were thought guilty and held responsible for the state of things. The blame was heaped so unreasonably and so often on the Rucks that they seemed to grow even taller and more indifferent to the people living under their shadow.

They were the town's least popular inhabitants, but there had been a time when they were almost unnoticed. Only when the jobs ran out and the yard grew silent were they noticed as if for the first time.

It was noticed how large they had grown and how, in the slightest of breezes, their black sides moulted thick clouds of dirt. They made you feel dirty just looking at them. It was noticed, too, how, when it rained, the water ran down them and formed a thick wash of sludge at their feet. Each year it was noticed how the wash of sludge edged closer to the houses directly beneath. Moreover, it was known that for all that they looked as if they could survive Armageddon, the Rucks were as stable as a house of cards.

Perilous to live under, painful to the eye, the symbol if not the cause of decay, Little Atherton had come to see all its ills reflected in the Rucks, but then it was a place and a time for exaggeration. When things were bad, the people of Little Atherton made them worse; it was a habit of theirs, a cock-eyed way of coping.

To the children, however, the Rucks were innocent

and much-maligned, like friends they were not supposed to play with. A God-given adventure playground, they played on them all day, and at night the Rucks figured in their dreams. They were a privilege. No other town had rucks the size of Little Atherton's. In a small town they gave them an idea of how big the world must be.

Children were always to be found up on the Rucks, even in school time, for what school inspector would travel way up there for truants? If one had, he would have found a few of them around the bottom, lighting fires. Others would be braving the sheer face and others, more timid, the back and slightly sloping side, climbing up to the flat top where the trampled slack glistened beneath the sparse thatch of unhealthy-looking grass.

Up on the Rucks was where they had their secret meetings, their ideas and their fantasy lives. Up there Batman fought with the Penguin and Luke Skywalker killed Darth Vader, boy-doctor examined girl-patient and Evel Knievel chased Wonderwoman on his Raleigh bike. Up there was where, one famous winter, Denise Monton had her famous fight with Deborah Ridley.

Chapter Two

Another Hole

It was a Wednesday afternoon early in February. It had rained all through January and everywhere was damp and soaking still. There was a thick wind blowing on top of the Rucks and the girls had to shout to make themselves heard for otherwise the wind whipped the words out of their mouths and carried them elsewhere. Shouting was fine by them. They were in a shouting mood.

'You said you were my best friend,' said Denise, a carrot-headed girl of twelve with a long, heavy face and the figure of a clothes prop. She pushed her fists down deep into the pockets of her orange woolly cardigan and stood with skinny legs apart, ready for anything.

Deborah, round-faced and round-bodied, in a baggy white dress and a red shawl she had borrowed from her mother that morning, tutted disgustedly.

'Honestly, Denise! Grow up, will you. You're like a kid, a big soft kid. Anyone would think you were about seven the way you carry on. Honestly!'

Deborah was the one with the power. She was the one you put your money on in a fight. She had that easy arrogance about her. It showed in her face, round and flat-featured except for the chin which jutted out like a doorstep, and in the aggressive swing of her blonde pigtails.

'You said you were my best friend.' Denise, the large, wide-spaced eyes downcast, was nearer than ever to tears.

'I am, I am! Honest! We were just playing, that's all. She had this pair of red high heels what she had for Christmas and I had this shawl from me mum this morning and we were just messing about and you weren't playing out anyway.'

'I was playing out.'

'No you wasn't.'

'I was.'

'Don't you pigging lie to me, Denise Monton, 'cos me and Simone Garner went to your house and your mam said you'd gone to the shop to get some Vicks for your dad's chest. So you weren't playing out. So there. So don't call us a liar or I'll pigging biff you one.'

Deborah stopped to readjust the red shawl about her shoulders and to pull it up at the back where its red-tasselled fringe was trailing in the mud.

'Anyway, she isn't me best friend,' Deborah cooed. 'Not me bestest friend.'

'Best friends is best friends.'

'Oh, put a sock in it, Denise. What do you think it is? God, can't even breathe without your say-so.'

'Best friends is best friends.' Denise's fists pressed so hard into her cardigan pockets that the pockets nearly catapulted off.

'Come off it a pigging minute. I'm nearly twelve. I'm too old for best friends.'

'You don't mess around with no one else, not if you're pigging best friends.'

'Says who?'

'Says me.'

'Says you? Oh pigging hell, must listen 'cos Denise Monton says so. Any road up, I weren't messing about.'

'You were.'

'I weren't.'

'Were.'

'Oh belt up, Denise, you crabby beggar. You make me sick. You think you're It.'

'I don't.'

'You do. You think you're It. You're not. You're shit. You're not even that when you're wiped up.'

The fists came out of Denise's pockets. 'You say that again and I'll knock your block off.'

'You and whose army?'

'I don't need no army with you.'

'Oh listen to Wonderwoman. Why don't you go home and use a can-opener on your grandad? I'd hate to have a grandad like that. He gives you the creeps.'

'Shut up about my granda' or I'll knock the smile off the other side of your face.'

'I've got something to smile about when I've a silly sod like you standing in front of me.'

The wind blew of a sudden. The gust bloated Deborah's white smock and wrapped Denise's green pencil skirt more tightly round her legs. It made Deborah seem large and powerful and Denise seem small and mean.

'I'm off home. I can't be doing with this. You get on me nerves these days, you really do.'

'Well bog off then.'

'I won't bog off. You bog off. Do you think I'm going to stand here and listen to you telling me to bog off? Do you? Do you? Then you've got another think coming. You bog off.'

'No.'

'You know what you are, don't you?'

'What?' asked Denise, fists ready, daring Deborah to say one word, just one word. 'What then? Go on, I dare you.'

'You're tapped, you are. You're tapped. You're a bit soft in the head.'

Well, that was it.

Quite simply, that was it.

Denise was not going to take any more lip from Deborah.

Lost for words and, God, she had it coming to her, Denise gave best friend Deborah one almighty shove, one even more almighty whack across the head. And, as Deborah fell under these blows, the earth yawned and in fell Deborah.

It looked funny at first. A complete and perfect circle of earth giving way under Deborah's feet, falling slowly at first like flour through a fine sieve and Deborah falling with it.

L.O.N.—2

It looked as if she had just parachuted down from the sky and landed in the sea with a splash. Then it looked frightening because this sea was not wet. It was black and did not splash but rose up in thick, choking clouds.

The dust spread and thinned quickly. People rushed out of their houses to see what that dirty big black cloud was doing up on the Rucks. An old mining shaft directly beneath the Rucks had given way. Little Atherton was notorious for them and it was well-known that the Rucks were a honeycomb of holes and tunnels inside.

When the first of the people reached the Rucks Denise was discovered, caked in dust but unharmed, sitting on the edge of a crater, her legs dangling in the sooty air.

'Are you all right, love . . .'

'. . . she looks all right . . .'

'. . . thank God . . .'

'. . . that's Denise Monton . . .'

'. . . I know her, goes to our school . . .'

'. . . lives by us she does . . .'

'. . . ambulance . . .'

'. . . on its way . . .'

'. . . any minute now . . .'

'. . . hurt . . .'

'. . . no bones broken . . .'

'. . . doesn't look like it . . .'

'. . . anyone with her . . .'

'. . . don't think so . . .'

'. . . doesn't look like it . . .'

'. . . take it easy . . .'

'. . . 's'all right now, you're all right now . . .'

'. . . on her own . . .'

A sea of words and disembodied voices swam through her head. She tried to see through the swathing clouds of dust but she could catch no sight of Deborah. Someone bundled her up in his arms and carried her down the slope to the waiting ambulance.

People stood about testing the uncertain structure of the Rucks by stamping their feet very tentatively and thanking God that no one had been killed, until someone noticed a scruffy red shawl dangling from a timber halfway down the hole that seemed to be as deep as the Rucks themselves.

Two hours later rescue workers found Deborah, buried six-feet deep under the slack at the very bottom of the hole, and hauled her crumpled golliwog of a body up into the bleak light of the closing day.

Chapter Three

The Montons

The oxygen cylinder clanked against Granda's iron skirt as she snapped it back into place.

It was a Wednesday, the same Wednesday, before Deborah fell to her dusty death. Mrs Monton always gave Granda' his all-over wash on a Wednesday. It meant separating him from the machine and lying him flat on the carpet in front of the gas fire. When she had soaped and rinsed his thin, flaking body she had then to reassemble him and the machine. It was a heavy task, and although she had the figure to match the task she had not the strength.

She rose, breathless, and steadied herself on two dumpy legs that were numb from kneeling.

'Tea?' she asked in a quiet, sing-song voice.

Her high Welsh accent had never left her although she had lived in Little Atherton some sixteen years now. Indeed, it was as strong as ever it was whenever she spoke to Granda'. She always spoke to him as if he were a child. She was no longer sure if he understood anything any more.

'I'll make us a lovely cup of tea, Granda', with lots of sugar to pep you up. I know you can always manage a good strong cup of tea.'

Granda' Jones, in reply, snapped and crackled like a bowl of Rice Crispies. Words were beyond him these days. He had developed a language of grunts, bubbles, pops and whistles that was suited to his needs. Mrs Monton and her family had come to understand it, for they knew his needs, which were few.

She turned from him and, with dull eyes, looked about the dingy front room. The room had known too many years and too few alterations. Things always needed fixing. Wasn't that another tear on the arm of the green vinyl settee? Wasn't the stuffing coming out of one of the fluffy yellow cushions? The carpets were worn and the wallpaper was discoloured and sad-looking. The furniture looked as if it had known better days. The whole house needed a good looking after. Mrs Monton had decided that many times but where were the money and the energy to come from?

Granda' whistled low and clear.

'Yes, I thought you'd like that. I knew a cup of tea would please you no end.' She smoothed out the white strands of hair that striped his pink skull and smiled tenderly. 'My poor old doll of a man. I know your ways of old. I know each one of them.'

Granda' Jones was her father-in-law from her first marriage, and was now past seventy and failing with the Dust. He'd first met up with the Dust in the slate quarries of Bethesda. It had made its nest in his lungs from the age of thirteen. By the time he was forty the Dust had so colonised and ravaged his lungs that even walking had become painfully impossible for him. His lungs were like lace and his flesh had wasted to a flimsy pink coverlet for his bones. Unable to lie down, for lying down trapped what little air his lungs could hold, he lived in and by means of an iron shell on wheels.

In design it was like a wheelchair with a canopy encrusted with dials, a breastplate and a skirt. He looked like a cross between a tank and an electric cooker. It hid most of his body from view, except for his arms, which hung lifelessly by his side. His face was covered by a pair of goggles – the light would burn his lids without it – and a breathing mask that was connected to an oxygen cylinder by his feet. This, his life machine, had effectively replaced his whole body, for those arms no longer functioned adequately. He could raise them with difficulty, but once raised they were too weak to do whatever it was they had been raised to do. Without the machine he would die. With it he was less than living, a dying dalek in the Montons' front room.

Mrs Monton sighed at the sight of him. She had been looking after him ever since her marriage to his son. Tending him, once that marriage had come to its short and rather ignoble end, had, she claimed, saved her from suicide. When she married Monton and moved North, Granda' had come with her. From his vantage point in the Montons' front room he had seen this marriage grow increasingly dull and the two grandchildren, Charles, his true grandchild, and Denise, the daughter by Monton, grow tall and un-Welsh.

What Granda' felt for his daughter-in-law no one could know. His vocabulary of burps and whistles was too limited to express his feelings. What Mrs Monton felt for him was gratitude – tending him had given her at least one purpose in life – and a deep maternal affection, deeper, though she would never have admitted it, than that which she felt towards her own children. Real children, she knew, had a habit of growing up and away from you. They grew cheeky and answered you back, and there came a day when you set out to slap them for it and they caught you by the wrist and you realised they were stronger than you. A poor investment, they never repaid in full the devotion a mother gave. Granda' Jones, however, was a true child, a helpless babe, and like every helpless baby he was a mirror, a mirror that reflected whatever was placed in front of it.

With a kiss to his wrinkled forehead, she left him and padded over to the window, her backless slippers slapping against the heels of her feet as she walked. She looked through the dingy net curtains, yellowed by the nicotine given off by a houseful of smokers, and out into the street where Denise, her daughter, was playing with her best friend, Deborah.

Mrs Monton, though broad and stocky, never gave the impression of being a strong woman. The violently tight curls of her fading red hair made an incongruous helmet for a face that was so long and uneventful. Her features – the tiny eyes, stooping brow and the soft and seemingly boneless nose – seemed reluctant to stand out against the rest of her face, and even her mouth, with its thin, streaky lips, sank well back from her chin as if cowering from a blow.

She turned from the window and looked regretfully towards the photograph of her eldest child, Charlie.

It stood in the far corner of the room. There was a slight recess just above the TV set and in it Mrs Monton had constructed an altar. The altar was a teak-laminated shelf and held a jar of paper poppies, a battered statue of Our Lady of Lourdes, a crucifix and the black-edged photograph of Charlie Jones Monton in army uniform.

Charlie had died, aged nineteen, on the streets of Belfast from a terrorist bullet, some four years previously. The bullet had entered his skull and he had died instantly. Now his petulant, grieved and slightly foolish face stared back at his mother, slyly reproaching her, or so she felt, for ever making him a member of such a blighted family.

Mrs Monton picked up the photograph and kissed it, the breath from her nostrils covering his image in a fine mist.

Granda' whistled deep and long.

'I know, Granda', I know. You want your tea. It's just that I miss him still.'

She sat down on the edge of the settee, took a dimp out of her apron pocket and lit it with the Martini-bottle lighter a neighbour had brought her from Spain.

'It seems to me,' she said philosophically, 'that we're fated, cruelly fated. Too many bad things have happened to us. We're like the Kennedys or the Barlows off *Coronation Street*. Tragedy stalks us.'

This was her favourite theme. It could rouse her to a passionate fury of rhetoric – for if Mrs Monton was

16

strong in nothing else she was strong in misery.

'Fated. There's my own mother dead in childbirth. Her sister, my aunt, gone the same way. Your wife, Granda', with the weak heart and the son she never saw walk, and her son, my poor Tom, gone to live in an early grave. May God bless each of them as much as they need it. Poor Tom. Time heals nothing, does it, Granda'.'

Tom had died of botulism. He alone had eaten the currant pudding his young wife had made to celebrate their third wedding anniversary and their son Charlie's first birthday. The currants were of uncertain age but were undoubtedly antique. She, having an abhorrence of them – they looked like rabbit droppings she had said – had not eaten any of the pudding. Granda' was on a liquid diet and the pudding was too rich for one of Charlie's years. Tom had eaten the lot, pronounced it the best pudding ever made and died painfully from it two days later. The cause of death made known to her, Gwen, out of one of the mad twists that grief spins, glutted herself on currants. Guilt and the hope that she would come across a similarly fatal batch drove her to it. For a month after the funeral she ate currants without rest. The Bethesda stores were ransacked for them and a trip to Bangor saw her return with two shopping bags full. Granda' – he'd had a voice then – finally persuaded her to stop.

'You're eating yourself into the grave, which is no fit place for a young woman with a fatherless child and an old man with the Dust hanging on her for their every need.'

Mrs Monton continued her list. 'And there's you, Granda', with the Dust – and if Tom had lived he'd have it too by now, and if Tom had lived we'd still be in

Bethesda and Charlie, doubtless, would be working in the quarry and the Dust would be dining on him as well. I've thought it all out. It's as if we're blighted whatever we do. Grief and misery stalk us wherever we go.'

The last was said with an eye to the photograph of Charlie, the dead Tom's only gift to an ungrateful world.

Mrs Monton was working herself up to a fine grief. She knew it, and stopped the flow of words in order to calm herself.

Life had not been so sweet in Little Atherton. Not as sweet as Monton had promised her. He had been a lorry driver and she a waitress. They'd met in the cafe where she'd worked. He had wooed and won her and taken her to Little Atherton. North Wales was a dead and a dying place.

'Bring Granda',' Monton had said. 'The air up North is grimy but it's sweeter, a darn sight sweeter. Bring Granda'. It'd do the old bugger good. And bring your Charlie too, of course. A young lad'll want to be where the opportunity is, and so'll his mother if I know her right.'

Monton had been a different man then, lively and persuasive. He hadn't consciously lied to her. He'd simply exaggerated. Little Atherton was a ghost town. It had little to boast of when she had first seen it sixteen years ago and it had even less now. Only the mills and the now disused railway yard broke up the ditch-like arrangement of slackheap and hobbled house. She'd hated the Rucks at first sight. She'd cried when she'd first seen the town, having expected a new Jerusalem, but took it as God's way and settled down with Monton, Granda' and Charlie. It was here that her daughter, Denise, was born, and it was here that she expected to live out her days.

'You know, Granda', we must have been terrible wicked to have deserved all that.'

Up until the death of Charlie life had been relatively quiet for the Montons. Monton was too work-shy to be in any danger of catching any industrial disease. Indeed, the only thing he'd ever suffer from, according to Mrs Monton, was bedsores. This was one of Mrs Monton's jokes. Mr Monton said it was her only one. He was a man who liked his sleep. Sleep was sensual and exciting, as nothing else in his life was, and he indulged in it at the slightest opportunity.

'He doesn't trouble me,' Mrs Monton was heard to say. It was a small blessing.

Denise did not trouble her overmuch either, which was another small blessing. She was clean and kept herself from trouble. The blessing, Mrs Monton suspected, could not last for long. Girls had a way of growing up that was made to wound a mother. This Mrs Monton knew for a fact.

You lose all respect for grief when it turns excessive. Life had not poured its riches unstintingly into Mrs Monton's lap, but only a bored and wasted mind could so firmly believe that God had picked her family to be prominent casualties of his vast and incomprehensible design. It was Charlie's death more than anything else that had brought her to this position. Life was a gloomy thing. You struggled against the worst in vain because the worst was all there was.

'I'll make that tea now.'

Granda' rasped a sigh of relief.

'Frank!' she yelled up to her sleeping husband. His muffled reply carried down the stairs and into the front room. 'Sleep, sleep, sleep. And what'd be done if it were me that was sleeping the whole day? Who'd get your tea then, Granda'?'

She leaned forward and flicked her ash into the ashtray on the mantelpiece and, with a heave, pulled herself up and padded back over to the window to call Denise in for tea.

Denise was no longer there. She and Deborah had disappeared. Her mother cursed her to hell for being so wayward and went into the kitchen to make the tea.

Although she busied herself in the kitchen, the sounds of water filling the kettle and pans and dishes clanking, Granda' was still without his tea half an hour later. He would not taste tea until much later in the evening, for he was about to be forgotten in the commotion caused when a neighbour came thumping at the back door to say that the Rucks had given way.

Chapter Four

The Mallet Memorial

Denise lay in a ward in the Mallet Memorial Hospital. She had arrived there giddy with shock and caked in dust. After she had given a policewoman a brief and unemotional account of the incident they had scrubbed her down, talked soothingly to her and, when she had complained of aches and pains down her spine and left leg, had promptly given her two shots of pethidine in either thigh before sliding her gently between two cool white sheets.

She did not so much sleep as float under a smooth darkness for two days after, and whenever she did wake, rising slowly through that smooth darkness, surfacing without a ripple, it was to the sad, high notes of her mother's voice as she talked or read the local newspaper to the woman in the next bed, a miserable streak of a woman with blue-grey hair, an orange wool nightie and a pair of leopard-skin slippers, slit up the side for the bunion. She was in for her bladder and her soul was a close sister to Mrs Monton's.

' "Fares War Takes New Twist as Bus Cuts Planned." Shocking the price of bus fares now, aren't they? Nearly a pound each way I paid to get here.'

'Six months since I was on a bus,' said the woman in the next bed. 'Six months lying here. I dream about going on a bus.'

'I know. Bladders are bad though, aren't they? Cripple you when they go wrong. "Youth Fined £100. A youth who used his father's motor cycle without his permission was fined one hundred pounds at Mallet on Tuesday." Our Charlie was keen on the motor bikes.'

Denise stirred behind her.

'Your girl's waking again,' the woman warned Mrs Monton.

'Mam?'

'Hallo, it's me, lovely. How are you feeling now?'

'I've been sleeping.'

'You've been sleeping ages and there's still sleep left in you. I have been here all this time to watch over you. Did you know that? Just me, just watching you lying there all peaceful. Your dad's with Granda', looking after him, and I am here with you, see.'

Denise moaned and slowly, gently rocked from side to side, disturbing the smooth sheets that her mother immediately resmoothed with the palms of her hands.

'Do you want anything, pet? There's grapes over by you and toffee sent from school. Everyone's worried for you.'

'Deborah?'

'Deborah's no more, lovely. We told you that.'

'Oh yes. I've been sleeping. It's been lovely, this sleeping and sleeping.'

'Well you go on and sleep some more. There's nothing for you to wake up to.'

Mrs Monton watched Denise turn and fall instantly to sleep, and then shared a sorry smile with the woman in the next bed.

' "Thefts from Cars," ' continued Mrs Monton. ' "A handbag, personal papers and a cheque book altogether worth forty-two pounds were stolen from an unattended car in Dorset Road, Roston." '

'You're in the papers a lot yourself, aren't you, Mrs Monton?'

'Sadly, we are. Yes, sadly. My husband buys all the papers every day, and someone he knows is videoing all the TV programmes. I don't read them. Too upsetting. And I'm not letting Denise see them either.'

'Right, quite right, quite right too.'

'But my husband is making a scrapbook, big, thick one it is, and when all this is over and not so upsetting we're going to sit down together and we'll read it as a family.'

'That sounds really nice.'

'There was nothing like this when our Charlie died. "Local Boy Shot Dead in Belfast." It was on the front page and pictures of the funeral on page four the next week.'

'I remember that.'

'Nothing like this. Seems like the whole world wants to

know about this and us and our Denise and that poor Deborah.'

'You're quite famous really.'

'If this is fame then it's a heavy thing and who would want it?'

Chapter Five

Sad Geography

When Little Atherton went into mourning the black and guilty face of the Rucks made an impressive funeral pall. There was in the town a tragic air, an air as thick as the dust that coated it. There was, too, that particular blend of anger and frustration that is present most especially when it is the young that are lost to us. The whole town grieved. This is no journalistic exaggeration. Everyone felt it to some degree. Grief was shared because the responsibility for her death was also shared. No one person was responsible for her death but it was the town itself, its sad geography.

The death of Deborah bowed heads low for many a day, none more so than the women's. They would stand and talk together and at length in shop doorways, at street corners and garden gates. They would talk of Deborah, of the deaths of children and the heartaches of parenthood. They spoke, too, of the criminal negligence of council, government and God for ever making them live under the shadow of the Rucks.

'They dump their dirt on us and leave us to live with it,' said one angry thin woman to another.

So they mourned and complained and felt the death of Deborah as keenly as one of their own.

Their children heard them and saw their adventure playground turn into what their mothers had always said it was, a death trap. They felt the breath of death whistle past. Deborah Ridley had been twelve years old. It wasn't just something that happened to you when you were old. It came to anyone, without warning, and not always in the dark but sometimes in the bright light of day. This was new to them and demanded serious attention. Nonetheless, whether because kids are callow and death a joke or because it was a way of coping with this mystery, a week later a new skipping rhyme was composed which began:

> Deborah Ridley
> She is dead
> She'll come back
> Without her head

They sang it in the streets, and when the women heard it they clouted them over the heads and said it was blasphemy.

The men propped up counters and contemplated tragic themes.

26

'Weren't it a good thing, though, when they closed down the yard and stopped working Overton pit?'

'Like hell it were. I haven't worked since. They left us with sod all when they did that.'

'I mean all the deaths they caused.'

'Still cause.'

'Aye.'

'Aye, even now.'

'Even now.'

'Shame.'

'Of course, I know him.'

'Ridley?'

'Nervous bloke. He'll take it bad.'

'They say how his wife is going doolally now and he's fast behind her.'

'Can you blame them though? I mean, can you blame them?'

'I know what I'd do. I'd unmantle them bloody Rucks with me bare hands. I'd do it for nothing, I'm telling you and I'm telling you now.'

'I know Monton too.'

'His girl lived though.'

'It's not the same somehow.'

'Lucky.'

'Still, shakes you up.'

'Mind you, Monton's a good bloke. Holds his beer.'

'Aye, sad times, sad times.'

Sad times indeed. In previous days, before the yard or the Rucks, when Little Atherton was a mess of fields and the hunting grounds of the Dukes of Bridgewater, the death of Deborah would have made up a folk song or two and Little Atherton was not yet so distant from its past that this folk element went for nothing. One could hear a cadence in the general talk, some barely discernible refrain, but, of course, though they had reached the place quickly, the television and the newspapers never quite caught it.

A TV camera had arrived almost immediately and had worked alongside the rescuers in retrieving Deborah's body from beneath the mud and slack. For the next fortnight or so newsmen crammed into Little Atherton, their presence giving off a whiff of excitement to mingle with the sadness. When one reporter called it 'a minor Aberfan' and wrote of a poor, benighted townsfolk miserable in their grief and angry at their neglect, a dubious but distinct pride glowed within them.

The people of Little Atherton loved the newsmen; they loved the attention they were given by them and, most of all, they loved Evan Weldon, later to find fame with his bulletins from Beirut and Kabul. His lengthy reports for the local TV were repeated, uncut, on the national news. It became for the rest of the country *his* story, so well did the fair and hungry-looking man with the soft and quietly impassioned voice describe the town and interview its inhabitants, asking their opinions as if they made a difference to the way he saw things. He had a habit, in those reports, of directing his camera accusingly at the Rucks before signing himself off. They made a good shot – the Rucks were nothing if not photogenic – but they also showed the people of Little Atherton that Weldon had listened to them, had followed their eyes as they spoke. He was everybody's hero. Little Athertonians clustered about his raincoated figure as he addressed the nation, gazing at the camera before them like primitives faced with their first Kodak.

It was in Weldon's reports that Deborah's face, round

and pink, veiled for her First Communion, flickered on every TV screen. He interviewed her schoolmates, each of whom were intent on declaring their best-friendedness with Deborah.

'We were dead close. She were a right laugh. We could kill ourselves laughing sometimes. We had the same sense of humour, laughed at the same things, made the same jokes, you know. We were what you call empathic,' said one girl, whose vocabulary was greater than her regard for truth.

It was to Weldon that the headmaster of Deborah's school had mumbled his appreciation of her particular gifts in needlework and history, one hand firmly clamped on his skull to prevent the wind that rifled through the school playground from lifting the carefully plastered hair from his bald patch.

Inside, the head led Weldon down the main corridor to where her particular gifts in needlework and history had helped Deborah in the re-creation through collage of the Bayeux Tapestry.

'We've put it up here, in the main corridor, because it is, well, let's face it, a difficult subject supremely well-attempted. Unfortunately, the main corridor is rather busy – dinner times, break times, change-overs, that sort of thing – and someone has ripped it up the middle here. But we have fixed it. You can just see the Sellotape. I think it shows promise, the promise, we think, that Deborah had within her.'

It was Weldon who managed a long and heart-breaking interview with the Ridleys. No one else in Weldon's business had received more than mumbled one-word replies and a few shell-shocked close-ups. Neighbours recommended Weldon to the Ridleys, saying that they had seen him on TV and that he was most empathic. The Ridleys did not find their neighbours to be liars. Weldon managed to elicit from Mrs Ridley a piercing and eloquent cry of maternal grief and from Mr Ridley a guided tour around the Ridley home. A small and shock-faced Ridley pulled open his dead daughter's bottom drawer and draped her no-longer-needed clothes about the bedroom, telling Weldon and the camera how each of these garments linked him up with a memory of his dear dead child. They extended the news for this report and the nation's TV programmes ran ten minutes late throughout the night.

Chapter Six

Snatching Joy

Everyone was full of Deborah. Denise was less in evidence. She was curiously neglected by the press, or so some thought. It was said that, not having managed to die, she was less interesting, but it was Mrs Monton who was responsible for her daughter's relative anonymity.

'Our family has known enough tragedy without splashing it nationwide,' she told a neighbour. 'Our Denise is upset enough. She's lost her friend and nearly her life. What good is it talking to them? It'd upset her more.'

Evan Weldon persuaded her otherwise.

'If people could see her on TV,' the soft voice disarming the mother completely, 'it would do the whole country good. We survive, Mrs Monton, we survive. We don't all go to the wall. Death does not conquer – not completely. Not if someone witnesses it and survives. That's what people will think when they see Denise. It will snatch a little joy from misery.'

Snatching a little joy from misery seemed such a rare and beautiful activity that Mrs Monton, her family's sad history in mind, said yes.

Denise was released from hospital. Mrs Monton collected her, and on the way home they stopped to buy Denise a frock and Mrs Monton a new blouse. Weldon was supposed to interview them that afternoon, but Denise was upset and cried a great deal and so the interview was postponed until the following day.

The interview began with the Montons, mother, father and a sullen Denise, grouped around Granda' underneath the photograph of Charlie. Then Granda' was wheeled out to the back kitchen to make room for the TV equipment, which packed the front room and spread out the door into the garden. Mr Monton joined Granda' in the back kitchen at his wife's insistence.

'He gets lonely by himself and they can't have him in here. There's no room and his breathing gets picked up on that microphone. Go on.'

'Let Dad stay, Mam. He's not doing nothing.'

'Exactly,' said Mrs Monton, 'which is why I want him in the back with your granda'. He can do nothing in there as well as he can do nothing in here, and more profitably too. Granda' 'll get vexed if he's by himself.'

'No matter, our Denise, I'll go. It's your mother's bloody show by the look of it.'

During the interview Denise and her mother sat on the settee, edgy and self-conscious, while Weldon, kneeling off-camera in the far corner of the room, questioned them about the tragedy.

'I feel great sorrow for Mrs Ridley. I had a son shot dead in Belfast for his country. I know what it is to lose a child. There's no loss like it. I lost a husband, too, and a mother and a father, but I could bundle their deaths together and it still wouldn't hurt as Charlie's does.'

'You seem no stranger to sad accidents like this, Mrs Monton.'

'Sadly, that's true. People have said to me, "Gwen, your family is like the Kennedys." We're Catholic, you see.'

'I see. Has your faith helped you these past few days?'

'Enormously,' she replied fiercely.

'And Denise? Has Denise been helped in this way? Have you, Denise?'

Denise did not answer. Her mother answered for her. 'My faith's my own. I've never put it on my own, not like some. I come to it to help me with my own life. I always hoped that my children would have no need of it. I always hoped they'd not have a life like mine.'

As her husband had intimated, Mrs Monton did most of the talking. Denise was less than forthcoming. All the while she sat, unconcerned, or so it seemed, lacing her fingers in her lap. It was on her, obviously, that the camera concentrated. It seldom left her. Even when her mother was talking the camera was trained on Denise. It began to annoy her, until she lost her shyness and became visibly cross with its rude stare. Her wide white eyes, the black pupils even further narrowed by the hot lights that flushed her face a salmon pink, bulged with bad temper. She kept silent until she heard her mother speak Deborah's name.

'Deborah? She and Denise were very good friends. They played all the time. She was a lovely, well-mannered, well-brought-up little girl.'

'You used to say that she was a cheeky madam, spoiled rotten.' Denise watched with interest as her mother's smile slowly froze.

'Denise?' Weldon asked, glad that she had finally spoken but wanting something more appropriate to the myth that was already rapidly forming around the dead Deborah. 'Could you tell us a little of what you remember of the incident?' He talked quietly, a slow whisper, as if she were a wild bird he wished to trap.

'We was playing up on the Rucks and we had an argument and we was fighting or nearly fighting anyway. Then I hit her smack on the head and she fell. Then the ground seemed to sort of open up, really. Deborah fell in and there was all soot about and dust and that, so that I couldn't see much else. That's it really.'

'You've obviously been affected greatly by all this, but how do you feel now?' His voice was as cool as milk from the fridge.

For a second she stared back at him as if she hadn't understood the question, and then she began to talk. She talked freely and with some feeling, but not about Deborah or the Rucks but about Granda'. Granda' was Welsh. He'd lived in Bethesda and had worked in a quarry. Granda' had the Dust and crackled when he tried to speak and had lungs like lace. He still hadn't had any compensation. Denise was very fierce on this point.

'They don't give it to you until you're dead, and not always then. They cut you up and say you had the Dust, but if you die from a heart attack or something, which most people do, then they don't give you compensation and anyway you're dead and what compensates you for that?'

Mrs Monton's hands fluttered about her face in embarrassment and the smooth flow of Weldon's sympathy was a trifle blocked by the irrelevance of Denise's reply.

'It's nerves, Mr Weldon, that's all it is. Denise, pay attention, will you? No one here wants to hear about your grandad.'

'Yes, Denise, it'd make a fine story for the news, but some other time perhaps. Now we're talking about Deborah. How do you feel about that now?'

Denise thought for a moment before replying. 'Not guilty,' she said finally. 'Not really guilty.'

A bushfire in Australia, the resignation of an American Vice-President and the arrest of a Hungarian trade unionist occurred simultaneously with Denise's interview and so only a portion of the interview was shown. Denise's plea of not guilty was not shown. If it had been, then the tide might have turned against the Montons even sooner than it did.

Chapter Seven

More Holes

The funeral was well attended by the people of Little
Atherton. The mayor, several councillors and other local
bigwigs also went, the vast publicity obliging them to.
What little work there was in the town ceased, and men
and women lined the dingy streets as the hearse passed
by slowly, jerkily on roads badly pitted by last year's
snow and still unrepaired.

At the cemetery the bright wreaths of white lilies and
the scarlet blazers of the secondary school choir stood out
against the black lake of mourners. The choir sang the
whole of the 'De Profundis' in uncertain Latin as

Deborah's coffin was lowered into another, smaller hole.

' "Out of the depths I have cried to thee, O Lord; Lord, hear my voice," ' the priest declared passionately, bringing out a section of the secondary school choir in a fit of giggles.

Denise was there. She and her mother stood with the rest of the mourners, unrecognized. She marvelled at the size of the crowd, the number of cameras and at the size of Deborah's coffin.

So small, she thought. She and Deborah had been the same size except that Deborah had been fat and she was thin. Perhaps death shrinks you up and you lose an inch or two. It seemed credible. The blood stopped flowing, the heart stopped beating, the lungs collapsed, everything settled down like the contents in a packet of breakfast cereal.

She could not feel moved in any way, although she realised that this was wrong and, looking at the weeping mourners all about her, peculiar to herself. It would have been easy to have forced a tear. She could cry at will. She and Deborah used to play at crying ages ago, seeing who could cry most, and Denise nearly always won – at that game anyway. She couldn't pretend to cry now because this was a real funeral, a really sad event, and it would be disrespectful to the memory of Deborah. She practised letting her mind go blank so that her face would follow suit and then people could read into her expression whatever they wished. She wouldn't have to think about what to feel then. It would be someone else's problem. The inside of her head felt as cold and as smooth as a mirror and her calm increased. She took her mind off the mourners and off Deborah and concentrated instead on the priest's head, watching the rain collect in tiny globules on his Brylcreemed hair.

The funeral over, Denise and her mother caught one of the specially laid-on buses back home, ate dinner, told Granda' in great detail about the funeral, ate tea, watched telly and then bed.

The next morning Denise rose early, dressed warmly and made her way through the waking town to the cemetery.

She was on her way to Deborah.

Why and what to say? She did not know. On waking she had been drawn there by a dim need to commune with her dead friend, perhaps to make peace with her.

The cemetery was deserted except for the birds. Sparrows flippered past on greased wings and a crow screeched in her ear as it flew by. A blue mist dragged the ground and frost sugared the headstones. It looked as a graveyard should look.

Deborah's grave was a disappointment. Denise had expected it to be neat and trim with a marble headstone bearing Deborah's name and dates and some suitable quotation from the Bible, like 'Eternal rest give unto them, O Lord, and let perpetual light shine upon them', or the one about death and its sting. It was a mean hole. It was a ditch filled up with soil muddy from the rain and streaked a dirty red with clay. The wreaths looked shoddy and lifeless. It hurt to think of Deborah lying under all that muck. How could she be at peace with a ton of dirt and rotting flowers weighing down upon her? Funerals were absurd and burials cruel. Surely there was a better way to cherish the dead.

'Perhaps I came a bit too soon,' she told the muddy grave, chatting to it like a friend, which was what it contained after all. 'Don't worry, Deb, they'll come and do you up today. Give you an headstone, too, as well. And if they don't, Deb, well, I'll come and see what I can do. I'll make it dead nice for you. I'll come every day, honest. I won't forget you. I'll come every week and we'll talk and I'll give you all the news. It'll be dead good. See you, Deb, see you.'

With that she turned and went back home, feeling pleased with herself and surprised at how pleasant it had been to stand and chat like that. It was like old times, and this way Deborah never got to answer back.

But that was the point, wasn't it? She didn't answer back. It was like talking to dolls, talking to the dead. It was just like talking to dolls when you were dead little. You could give dolls whole lives. You could think of them as almost real. But they weren't real, and Deborah wasn't real – not any more. Once she was real and then she wasn't. Once she was there and then she wasn't. Death was like that, she saw. Death was something which created holes, gaps where life used to be. Didn't Nature abhor a vacuum, though – some dim memory of a science lesson came to mind? In that case, wouldn't Nature fill up the hole? Surely you couldn't let all these holes just lie about unplugged or unfilled for either death would leak in or more life would leak out.

By the time she reached home she was cross and confused with all this thinking, the way it made you prove a point and then disprove it, leaving you back where you were.

She kept her graveside visit a secret. No one ever guessed she'd been there except Granda', who saw her sneak back into the house that morning. Despite her vow, she never visited the grave again.

Chapter Eight

To The Left

The death of Deborah was either to be a turning point or simply a sad episode in Denise's life. She did not believe it was up to her to decide which. She did not pass judgement on her own life. Her initiative was flabby from lack of exercise. She waited for life to signal how she was to react to it. She was obedient and sensitive to the wishes of fate.

This was not her mother's way. It is a mother's way to watch and worry and, in particular, it was Mrs Monton's way. Mrs Monton considered life to be an odd and dangerous possession, like having a pet cobra in the kitchen. You had to watch it carefully in case it wrapped itself around your legs when you were carrying a tray piled high with your best tea service. Cups and saucers had lain broken at her feet once too often.

'She's quiet. She's quieter today than she was yesterday,' her mother would observe of Denise. 'She was quiet yesterday, too. It's an odd quiet, not like a proper quiet. It's not a nice, lazy quiet. It's a thinking quiet.'

'So? She's always been quiet,' her father would reply, but he was inexpert at appreciating the many types and qualities of quiet. Like his daughter, Monton did not pass judgement on life, and if his daughter's initiative had grown flabby then in comparison his had atrophied years ago. He did not even wait for life's signals and was ignorant of the wishes of fate.

'She's too quiet. The wrong sort of quiet. She sits there looking at that telly with that soft look on her face. It's not right.'

'She's always done that. Our Denise wouldn't say boo to a goose, and well you know it. She's a good girl. Leave her be, Gwen, for God's sake, just leave her be.'

Mrs Monton would not leave be.

'You're very quiet, our Denise. You're not thinking things are you? Don't think things. Whenever you're thinking, let your mind go blank.'

'I weren't thinking. I were just sitting here doing nothing,' Denise replied tetchily.

'You've had an ordeal. I can see why you might be quiet, but I know you, Denise. You're like me, you are. You brood, Denise, you brood on things and that's bad. Brooding's bad and I know you're brooding because, you see, you've been so quiet of late.'

'God, you'd get at me if I weren't quiet. You can't do

nothing in this house but you get moaned at for it.'

Mrs Monton kept Denise off school for a fortnight after the funeral. She said she wanted to make sure that Denise was all right. She was worried about the girl and said that she was not the same somehow. She would have kept her off indefinitely had not a social worker in a pink Crimplene suit and a paisley headband visited the house and made light of her fears and insisted on Denise's prompt return.

She brought Denise into school late the next day and left her there only after she had heard the most profuse reassurances from the head that Denise would be closely observed, watched for any sign of disturbance and sent home immediately if any were seen.

It was strangely odd that first day back at school. It was as if she had been off years, not weeks. Walking around, in classrooms and in the playground, she felt herself being watched furtively by everybody. Being the object of such attention made her feel giggly and important. She quite liked it. She liked the way everyone was reserved and polite, even the fifth-year boys, and the way everybody made a point of trying not to mention Deborah's name to her.

'God, I hate French,' one girl, Dawn Cole, said to her outside the language lab. 'It's dead boring.' She stopped abruptly, slapped her hand over her mouth and said, 'I'm ever so sorry, Denise. I mean it's very boring, very boring indeed. Oh, I wish I hadn't said that. I wish the earth'd open up and swallow me. Oh fuck, I don't mean that neither.'

A respectful silence in such conditions cannot last too long and, in fact, it was Dawn Cole who broke it the next day. Sitting on a fence during break, working hard on a

42

piece of chewing gum, she asked, with false idleness, what it had been like.

'What was what like?'

'Oh go on, Denise. You know what I mean. What were it like? Were there blood? Janice Evans said there must have been because her boyfriend, Kez Hughes, said his brother were there and he said they had to carry her down the Rucks in two black plastic bags. He said that Deb had been broken in half. I wanted to go but our mam wouldn't let us. What were it like really?'

'I didn't see much because they took me away in an ambulance.' As Denise said this she noticed how disappointment altered Dawn's eager expression.

That look set her thinking. She had been involved in a real death, had been in the newspapers and on television. Those people not jealous of her thought her a star. Deborah's death had given her glamour and a reputation to which she was expected to live up. When asked to describe what had happened, she soon learned to tell it in a way that would encourage them to ask again. With a fine and intuitive knowledge of her audience, she began to realise that the true objective of telling a tale was not to inform but to entertain. The Death of Deborah became her party piece. She could win friends and attention with it. Of course she embroidered it a little.

Sometimes she told it, as she said, 'dead romantic'. Deborah, a fated girl, madly beautiful, with an obsession for the bleak attraction of the Rucks where she had once met a man as dark and as rugged as the Rucks themselves, a man who had taken her in his arms, held her tight against his broad chest and – raining hot passionate kisses upon her face, shoulders and quivering body – had turned her into a woman.

'He left her lying on the wet grass with tears in his soft brown eyes and the promise that one day he would return, that one day he would call and she would hear and they would be together till the end of time. Four Eva Two Geva — Four Always. For a fortnight after she walked round like a zombie. Do you remember?'

Her audience would of course remember.

'Yeah, she had this far-away look in her eyes and she kept being told off in maths.'

'That was because her mind was always on him. She were obsessed with him. She didn't know his name so she called him Wayne 'cos that was her favourite boy's name. She told me everything 'cos me and her were best mates. And then one day, right, she came up to us and she goes, "Denise," she goes, "Denise, I can hear him calling me and I must go to him," and then she ran off to the Rucks. I didn't catch up with her until we were right on top of the Rucks and there was this dirty big hole there that I'd never seen before and she was standing right on the edge of it. She turned to me and she looked at me and she goes, dead quiet like, "Goodbye, Denise," and I called out to her not to jump. I goes, "Don't do it, Deb, don't do it!", almost screaming it, and then she sort of fell into the hole. I watched her body plummet through the darkness straight down to the arms of her love.'

'Of her love,' would come the echo from one of the more-absorbed members of her audience.

At other times, depending on her audience again, the story would change from the romantic to the horrific. In that version Denise and Deborah would be up on the Rucks playing with an ouija board and celebrating a black mass to call up Hanratty.

44

'He was a famous mass murderer. Killed loads of people. Loads. Deb was mad keen on Hanratty. She'd seen all about him on this programme on telly. She knew his life as well as you or me know our way to school. She kept his picture under her pillow at night so he could be in her dreams and give her secret messages and she wrote his name all over her school books. Anyway, right, we were up on the Rucks for a séance. Deb was dying to contact him, you see, and I were dead scared of what were going to happen. We kept saying his name again and again dead quick. "Hanratty! Hanratty!" we were going, and then, no kidding, the ground opened up. I were dead scared, but Deborah, she were laughing and giggling like she'd never been so happy in her life, like as if she were drunk. So anyway, there was this big hole and there were great gobbets of black smoke coming out of it and flames an'all and Deborah toppled right in and you could hear the flames lick the flesh off her bones and her screams pierce your skull.'

'Was it Hanratty?'

'No, it were the milkman. Who do you think it was?'

No one believed that Denise's stories were an accurate account of what had happened up there on the Rucks but they were happy to be persuaded that they were. There were, of course, cynics in her audience, doubters, carpers, people who looked for a rip in the fantasy so that they could tear the tale in two and make Denise look a fool.

'I heard about Hanratty, too, and what I heard was that he were really innocent and it were really someone else what done them crimes and not him at all.'

'Well, there's no smoke without fire,' Denise had replied. She must have known even then that innocence was irrelevant, that death, violent death, involvement with it, leaves a stain that never fades and people come to recognize you for that alone.

The stories depended on her mood, her audience, what she had seen on television the other night. What each version had in common, of course, was Denise, Deborah and the fact that they were only very lop-sidedly constructed on the truth; only Denise's presence at the moment of Deborah's death was actual, the rest, leaning well to the left of reality, slipped into fantasy. Fortunately for Denise, her story-telling was admired but not believed. None of her friends thought her the least bit odd or morbid for telling them. Denise saw nothing in them that was harmful to anyone. After all, they weren't true.

Mrs Monton never heard any of these stories, nor did she ever hear of her daughter's fame in telling them, despite the fact that, in her search for mental scars, her vision was near-microscopic.

At night Mrs Monton would sit up in bed, the light on, chain-smoking, pondering on her daughter's well-being.

'She's come through it fine, Gwen,' Monton would moan, pushing his head deeper into the pillow. 'She's just fine. Let her be.'

Chapter Nine

A Burst of Lace

The death of Deborah had caused both Little Atherton and Denise to be thrown before the national gaze for more than a month, but the event, in itself, seemed neither large nor traumatic enough to scar either of them forever. In fact, if anything, they both appeared to thrive on it.

Representatives of a Japanese car firm visited the country with the much-publicised intention of building a plant somewhere in the United Kingdom, possibly Little Atherton. Once more, TV cameras and reporters descended on the town and crowds gathered as black-suited

Japanese walked about the H_RR_ _YAM_ ARNDAL_ CENTR_, inspected the waste ground that had once been the yard and praised Northern warmth and industry.

There was much talk and great hope engendered by their visit, for this was a town in which the words 'work' and 'wages' were in danger of disappearing from the language. The death of Deborah, the media glare and the promise of employment all gave the town a renewed sense of purpose. There was a hope of resurrection for the dead town. The future seemed once again a possibility.

The *Mallet Observer* initiated a campaign, called 'Little Atherton 2,000', where readers were invited to send in suggestions that would not only renovate the town but also transform it into a place 'where tomorrow happens today'. Week after week they printed drawings by children of sky-scrapered cities with mile-high pathways and flying cars. There were regular letters that detailed how Little Atherton could be turned into the town of tomorrow by all manner of crazy schemes.

These dreams for the future were all nourished by the prospect of the Japanese car plant. Plans were announced, a model of the proposed plant was set up in the library and a site on the waste ground that had once been the yard was fenced off in readiness. But somehow the plant never did get itself built. It just seemed to be forgotten, as was the town itself, and, for a while, Deborah too.

Denise enjoyed the sensitive treatment she received. The teachers spoke quietly to her and made sure that she was always involved in class activities. Girls jostled and, on one occasion, fought each other to take the absent place next to Denise that Deborah had once occupied.

As interest in Deborah's death and Denise's renditions

of it faded, Denise slowly and pleasurably began to find that she could be liked for herself and not just as Deborah's shadow. Nowadays she seldom walked home alone. She had never known such success. She loved the attention that other people gave her. She grew vain and a little callous because of it.

Only her mother's worrying ways irritated her. No day could pass without some comment upon her condition.

'You're too thin . . . you don't eat . . . you're too quiet . . . you're laughing too much these days. Giddy laughing. Laughter soon turns to tears.'

She could hear such comments at night, too, when, if she was unable to sleep, she would put a glass up against the wall and listen in on her parents' conversation – or, rather, her mother's monologue for her father never seemed to reply above a grunt.

'She was looking up at them Rucks again . . .'

'. . . she could spend all day looking up at them Rucks if you didn't stop her when you caught her at it . . .'

'. . . and she's so sly about it, too. Pretends she doesn't know what you're talking about. Looks at you as though it's you that's daft . . .'

'. . . don't you bother about her, Frank . . .?'

'. . . I suppose I bother about her enough for both of us, but then I have to. If I were to leave you to do the bothering then it would never be done and must you wear those socks in bed . . .?'

'. . . she's dull about the eyes . . .'

'. . . there's no more flesh on her than would do Sunday dinner . . .'

'. . . I worry about her. I worry. With Charlie gone what else is there for me to do? With Charlie gone what else have we? What else to hold us together . . .?'

'. . . there's Granda', of course. There's always Granda' . . .'

'. . . have you noticed how thick she is of late with Granda' . . .?'

Denise had indeed become thick with her granda', and suddenly too. Previously she had ignored him. It had been easy to look on him as part of the furniture. And not simply because he had been in the house – immobile and helpless, encased in metal from toe to top – for as long as she could remember, but also because, in his machine, he looked less like a human being than a piece of modernist furniture, shiny, angular, metallic and at odds with the soft, dumpy sofa, the lace antimacassars and tiny ornaments that cluttered and cosied the Monton's front room. Only his grey and liver-spotted hands, their long, thin fingers fluttering and unfurling about his lap, seemed even faintly human. It was understandable, then, that Denise had for so long ceased to think of him as a member of her family and as something that was washed and scrubbed and replenished regularly like the Calor gas stove.

She took to looking after him. Coming home from school it was to him she went first, and at weekends she took to sitting with him for hours at a time, attending to his few needs, wheeling him around the front room, kitchen, and the little patch of garden at the back. She even helped bathe him and never once blushed or felt strange scrubbing down a naked man, but then, stripped for the moment of his machine, Granda' looked even less human; a shrivelled skeleton bound tightly in flaky white leather. Evenings she would curl up against him, leaning against the cold metal skirt, and listen to him shuffle his legs against its walls as she watched television.

'Granda',' she'd say, reading out of the paper to him, 'you can watch a documentary on Arabs on ITV, or *Horse of the Year* on BBC-1 or a play called *In the Winter of Our Lives* on BBC-2.'

'What are you telling him that for?' her mother would ask.

'Nowt wrong with it. Why shouldn't I?'

'You know full well that he doesn't understand one half of what you're saying.'

'He can see me lips move.'

'I doubt he can even do that, pet, he's so far gone.'

'Don't say that in front of him.'

'And why shouldn't I say what I like? Very protective all of a sudden, aren't we?'

'You what?'

'Very thick with your granda' all of a sudden.'

'What if I am?'

'I wish you were as caring with me and your dad.'

'What have I done now? I haven't done nothing.'

'I never said you did, did I?'

'God, I hate this house. You get picked on for nothing.'

'I'm not always picking on you, Denise. I am too free if anything, and well you know it.'

'Y'are. Always picking on everything I do.'

'Nonsense.'

' 's true.'

'Then why so thick with your granda' all of a sudden? Why all lovey all of a sudden with him? Look at you. Go look at you now. You're wrapped around his legs like a ribbon round a parcel and don't you deny it because you can't.'

'I like the way he whistles.' As if on cue, there came a

51

slow high whine and a pop and a crackle of air rose up from Granda's Dust-corrupted lungs. 'It's like bird song. You sound like a canary, don't you? Funny but have you never noticed how you never hear him in the dark?'

'I don't know if you're cracked or stupid, Denise. I hope you're just stupid for your own sake.'

Although she would never have admitted it, not even to herself, Mrs Monton was waiting for Granda' to die. It would be best for him – what life was it for him anyway? Lungs like lace and they say it's infectious. They say they spill it out into the air when they breathe. Perhaps Denise should not sit so close.

Mrs Monton did not have much longer to wait. The one large burst of air that was needed to rip his ragged lungs apart came one Sunday morning. Denise was wakened by her father shouting up the stairs to her mum. His yell had broken through a dream of Deborah, of Deborah falling.

Another name was added to the family's casualty list and another body to the family grave; Granda' Jones joined his son and grandson Charlie in the little cemetery in the sharp and freezing canyons of Bethesda in the north of Wales. The funeral mass was held there, too. Little Atherton had never really been his home. He'd not been out into it above a dozen times. There was a small gathering – Mr and Mrs Monton, Denise, a preacher and a gravedigger – for few remember to attend the funerals of the already-long-dead.

Denise had never set foot in North Wales before. In the cemetery, she looked about at the tiny cottages and the short and crooked rows of terraced houses and up at the crags of slate which towered over the village, and she was struck with its resemblance to Little Atherton.

Her mother also saw the resemblance, had long noticed it. Bethesda was her native town. She knew each street of it and each hill and slate tip, had walked along them enough as girl and woman. She knew that all born and living there never lost the grey lining the air gave to the lungs, and she knew that the children of Little Atherton had lungs of a similar shade, and it was in that as well as in the landscape that she saw similarities.

'The air itself is poisoned. It's as if we begin dying as soon as we begin to live.'

'Oh belt up, you miserable cow,' said her husband. He did not like funerals. Funerals made you think and no good came from too much of that. He felt we'd all be better off without funerals. A man should come round and cart of the corpse in a van and life should go on. There was too much ceremony about death. 'Why do you always look on the black side of things anyway?'

'Because we're at a funeral. What other side is there to look at?'

When they returned home they took their grief in different ways. Monton slept longer and heavier than usual and Mrs Monton wandered about the house and garden, dazed and at a loss. The family's resemblance to the Kennedys grew greater in her mind and she stopped going to church. What help had becoming a Catholic ever been? It hadn't given her or her family any greater protection. Mrs Monton grew sullen and argumentative towards the God who had come late into her life and had failed to make much difference to it. In turn, Denise, the daughter who had also come late into her life and who had also failed to make much difference to it, grew increasingly more sullen and argumentative towards her.

'She's taking it bad. You can only take so much. What

with Granda' and Charlie and Deborah. I don't know how to take it and I'm an old woman nearly. My poor daughter.' So would Mrs Monton speak to herself when cooling down after a long hot argument with Denise over some trivial thing.

Denise cried every time she sat in the front room, oddly bare and characterless without Granda's contraption – sold in Bethesda to another Dust sufferer – and silent, too, without his counterpoint of harsh cough and soft whistle. The house was a shell without him. It was strange that a man whose existence had been so peripheral could make his absence felt so strongly.

One afternoon, barely three weeks after the funeral, the phone rang. Monton was alone in the house and he woke from a deep sleep to answer it. Sleep addled his brain and he followed the speaker's thread with difficulty.

'Hallo.'

'Hallo.'

'Mr Monton? Am I speaking to Mr Monton?'

'Yes, that's me.'

'Mr Stead here . . .'

'Who?'

'Mr Stead. Of Cut Price Supermarket.'

'Cut Price? Yeah, so? What do you want?'

'Yes, I'm the manager here and I'm ringing to say that we've got your daughter.'

'Our Denise? What's she doing there? She should be at school.'

'Yes, she's here with me in the office.'

'Shoplifting. She's been shoplifting.'

'No, no, not shoplifting.'

'Well, I'll bloody string her up if it were shoplifting.'

'Well, she's quite innocent. She is upset. That's why she's here.'

'Upset? How do you mean? What's up with her?'

'She's calmed down now. We found her crying at the check-out tills.'

'I see.'

'She was very upset.'

'Ah, you see her grandad's just died recently. They were very thick with each other, very close, you see.'

'Oh really, I'm sorry to hear that, I really am.'

'Well, thanks. I'll come over and pick her up.'

'Oh, do so, yes. But, Mr Monton, I'm sorry to hear about her grandad and I'm sure it's all related but I don't think she was upset about him exactly.'

'Oh?'

'Well, she was calling after someone, a girl, a girl called Deborah. It seems they went shopping together and your Denise lost sight of her and then we found her crying. And now she says this Deborah is dead. That's not the same Deborah that died up on those Rucks, is it?'

Chapter Ten

A Few Boomerangs

The change, so long looked for and feared by Mrs
Monton, was sudden and intense. From the day her
father dragged a tearful Denise home from Cut Price
Supermarket and walloped her for being so daft she was
never, her mother claimed, the same again.

A smack on the face proved to be the only effective way
to deal with Denise's tantrums – about three a week.
Monton would deliver the necessary blow. He had a
wide, flat palm, made for smacking. Mrs Monton could
only cover her face with an apron whenever Denise
began to scream and pound on the walls because she

wanted to watch ITV and her parents were watching BBC, or because they were eating fish and they had had fish the week before and why should she eat the same crap as they did anyway. The smack would shut her up pretty sharpish, but one night Denise smacked her father back and the next day her mother pushed through a crowded waiting room and demanded that the doctor do something. The doctor wearily wrote out a prescription for a bottle of mild tranquillisers.

'They wouldn't do much for you or me but for a girl your daughter's age they should be enough. It sounds like puberty. Girls get like that. It'll pass. Do you want some tranquillisers yourself?'

Denise refused to take the tranquillisers and, as neither parent fancied force-feeding her, the smack was once again used – but from then on Monton made sure his left was ready to defend himself.

The language she used in her tantrums was shocking, and of a type never heard before in that house, but if the swearing and the temper shocked her parents the casual lies she began to tell shocked them more. She would rather lie than be truthful about the smallest thing.

'Have you washed your face this morning?'

'Yes.'

'Doesn't look like it.'

'Well I have.'

A trip upstairs would reveal a face-cloth as dry as cardboard. The face-cloth would be dangled accusingly. Denise would lie again and claim that she had used her hands, or would slide into another blood-hot tantrum. There seemed to be no great shame in being caught out in this lie or any other. Truth, it seemed, like Charlie, like Deborah, like Granda', was just another casualty.

The school, too, had noticed the change in Denise. She was suddenly remote and dull in class, aggressive in the playground and stroppy with the teachers. It was pointed out that losing a friend and losing a relative were never easy, especially if you were a teenager. Adolescence was always a trying time and a close association with death would not make it any easier. Denise was controllable as yet. They would play it by ear – and soon school would be breaking up for the summer anyway.

The last week of term, six weeks after the Cut-Price incident, saw Denise grow odder. Miss Sweeney had begun her lesson with a little work on antonyms and synonyms.

'Remember, Thirds,' she cooed, 'that an antonym is a word opposite in meaning to another word. Light and dark are antonyms, as are . . . Well, can anyone tell me any interesting antonyms?'

The class told her a few and Miss Sweeney breathlessly thanked them for their cleverness and generosity, and did so again when offered a batch of synonyms. She moved on to a related comprehension and felt happy. The lesson was mundane, yes, but well-planned and executed. She felt that she had taught them something. At the end of the lesson she asked them once again what a synonym was and what an antonym was and received correct answers to both questions. She noticed, however, that Denise Monton looked rather vague and decided to test her.

'Denise, what is an antonym? I want to see if you've been listening.'

Denise looked up at Miss Sweeney with the lost and fearful stare of one who has been wakened from a deep sleep by being thrown into an ice-cool pool. Miss

Sweeney calmly repeated the question. Denise, floundering, answered, 'It's a bird.'

The class erupted. Laughter broke out loud enough to rattle the walls. It wasn't that funny but the latest fashion was to laugh like a drain at every possible opportunity. The blood shot to Denise's head and positively banged about in it.

'Shut up!'

They didn't; even Miss Sweeney indulged in a silvery snort behind her hand.

'Shut up or I'll kill you.'

This did not do the trick. Only Miss Sweeney stopped, the rest of the class doubled the decibels.

'Kill us all, would you? Tough nut Monton there.'

'We're really scared, Denise.'

'Hard case Monton there.'

'That's enough, Thirds. Sit down, Denise. You've already made a fool of yourself. That's enough for one lesson.'

'And you, Sweeney,' Denise declared threateningly.

'Run, Miss, she means it.'

Miss Sweeney did not run. The thought of running never crossed her mind – a mind occupied with the question of whether she should deal with the chaotic class first or the manic Miss Monton.

'I've already done one,' said Denise, licking her finger and drawing a figure one in the air and licking it again to score the figure out with a diagonal stroke. She licked the finger again and was poised to make another figure. 'Do you want to be number two?'

Neither Miss Sweeney nor the class was impressed by the threat. Denise was not a threatening figure, too skinny and sullen. Miss Sweeney banged on the desk with her board duster and called for order from behind the resulting cloud of dust. The calls for order were ignored but the bell for break was not. The class fled from the room at the sound of the bell, Denise leading the way. Miss Sweeney hurried to the staff room to inform her colleagues of Denise's behaviour.

In the yard, Denise separated herself from her friends, who were doing imitations of the Antonym Bird, and sat in the toilets. When the bell went, she didn't. She stayed there until dinner time.

In the dinner queue Dawn Cole came up and asked what she had meant when she had said that she had killed Deborah. That was what Denise had said, wasn't it?

'You said it were an accident.'

'I was lying.'

'You shouldn't joke about things like that.'

'Why not?'

' 'Cos it's in bad taste.'

Summer came the next week, school broke up and the Antonym Bird was forgotten – but Denise's claim to have killed Deborah Ridley was not.

Denise stayed in the house all summer and watched telly all day. She would break away from the telly only to lie to her parents, throw a tantrum and lock herself in her room or sunbathe in the tiny back garden, a transistor, full volume, inches from her ear. When friends called for her she would either refuse to come to the door or, when she did come to the door, tell them to get lost. She was fourteen. She was too old for friends.

When school began again – the Montons thanked God for the six or seven hours of peace it guaranteed each weekday – Denise told everyone the same thing, whether or not they were interested: she had killed Deborah Ridley.

'Denise, you couldn't kill a dead sheep,' said Dawn Cole.

Denise's desire to be known as a murderess was treated as an attempt to gain attention. Some girls fall in love with pop stars, some take drugs, others get a reputation for sex, Denise wanted to be known as a murderess. It was decided to ignore her claims or treat them humorously – but to starve this desire was only to increase it.

Denise began to scribble on desks and exercise books. She would spend her time in lessons inking over graffitti such as, 'Denise and Deborah', 'Den and Deb', 'Deb is dead, long live Den' and 'Den & Deb 4Eva2Geva'.

She refused to write in any ink other than black – *in memoriam*.

'Avoid confrontation,' said the head. 'It's what she wants. Don't give it to her.'

In her essays for Miss Sweeney there would always be something of Deborah: in 'A Day Out' it was a day by the sea with Deborah, Deborah paddling; in 'If I Ruled the World' Denise would direct all scientists to work towards bringing Deborah back to life; and in 'A Childhood Memory' there was Deborah falling to her death. 'Trapped in a Lift', 'A Day in the Life of a Penny', 'Gardening: Chore or Pleasure?' – Deborah could always be slotted in. Miss Sweeney began to find herself planning lessons around potentially Deborah-less topics but was at a loss. It seemed that every piece of work that asked for imagination or opinion could feature a Deborah; a Deborah who was beautiful, wealthy, loved by all and nearly always dead by the end of it.

Her teachers' exasperation grew and their tempers shortened as Denise's obsession deepened.

'It's getting severe, this Deborah thing, you know.'

'Snap out of it, Denise.'

'Denise Monton, you go too far and that's always been your trouble.'

She was always being asked to stay behind to be lectured on her behaviour, her lack of concentration, on pulling herself together, on not wasting herself – and too often the teacher's attention would stray and fasten on to the filth in which Denise was choosing to live, for she had given up washing herself. She washed only if her mother dragged her to the sink and scrubbed her struggling daughter with a soapy flannel. Denise preferred to search through the laundry bag for an odd pair of dirty socks or a blouse with a grimy collar than wear the freshly washed and ironed uniform her mother laid out for her.

'What must they think of you in that school and me who's responsible for you? What must they think?'

'She's thick,' said the music teacher.

'She's not thick,' said the maths teacher, 'she's stupid.'

'She's not stupid,' said Miss Sweeney, 'she's sick, clinically sick.'

Ignoring what were seen as her attempts to gain attention allowed them to continue unabated and so, finally, Denise was seen by an educational psychiatrist. There were several visits, each one taking place in the nurse's room in the school, three with Denise, one with her parents and one with all three. They were all on a level of a quiet chat. Denise enjoyed them and talked lucidly and openly to the man. Seeing him, she felt her claims had been taken seriously at last and, also, that that they were now seen to be justified.

Mr and Mrs Monton positively buckled under the shame of it, but Denise blossomed anew. Her books were backed with new wallpaper and remained as immaculate as her school uniform. Her behaviour and her concentration returned to normal, satisfactory standards. The school had been right all along, all Denise wanted was attention, and Mrs Monton found herself happy that Denise had been cured so quickly and so easily.

'Cured? Oh, dear no,' said the man. 'She is obsessed by the memory of that girl and she still believes that she's responsible for her death.'

But it had been an accident. There was no question of it being anything else.

'Well, the mind always questions, doesn't it? Look at it this way: she and the girl had been fighting, shoving each other, Denise's temper rising; she wants to kill her, for a moment she really does, and, at that moment, the Rucks decide to cave in on the precise spot where she is standing. Deborah falls, Deborah dies and Denise wanted it to happen. A sad coincidence, an amazing coincidence, but there we are.'

As he spoke he walked around the seated Montons in dizzying and imperfect circles with the elegant and balanced gait of a dog on its hind legs. Sits behind a desk all day, thought Monton, explaining the man's walk to himself.

'There's no guilt there. She simply wants it to be accepted as fact. Your daughter is very stubborn and won't be persuaded otherwise. But children, even adolescents, they get strange ideas and they stick with them in the face of all the facts. When I was young I believed electric lights used up the daylight and the more people used them the darker it got. It made sense to me, and

Deborah's death makes sense to Denise. She'll either grow up and forget it or grow up and laugh about it.'

There was little to be done with Denise. Apart from continually insisting that she had killed Deborah Ridley, she became again the satisfactory pupil and the sullen but dutiful daughter. Nothing more could be done. She could not be put into care; she had a good home and loving parents and hospital would be an over-reaction to what was a minor *idée fixe*.

Things came to a standstill.

For Denise it had become blindingly simple. There was the angry shove. There was the world physically collapsing as if on cue. Denise had wanted Deborah dead and the very earth had conspired with her in satisfying this desire. The Rucks had been her accomplice and her weapon.

Again and again, naturally, casually, matter-of-factly, but never again with that driving insistence, she would pit her conversation with phrases like, 'that was before I did Deborah in' and 'me and Deb, that's this girl I killed once'. Eventually, people hearing these phrases began to believe her, despite themselves.

Friends were no longer as friendly and neighbours not so neighbourly. Little Atherton stood back and looked at her suspiciously, this red-haired girl, red hair equals temper, the fishy eyes in the pale, white face, and thought, well, who knows, who knows what did happen up there on the Rucks, just the two of them. Deborah, being dead, was easy to imagine as victim, angel, and Denise, strange and slightly touched, the survivor of the two, assailant, devil.

Chapter Eleven

A Town Not Big Enough

DENISE MONTON IS A MURDERER ran the legend on the school wall, scrawled in suitably red chalk that the rain never did quite wash away. The wall looked out onto the main road. Denise could see the heads of people turn to read it as they went past. A similar message, written with an aerosol can, again in red, was sprayed on the walls of the H_RR_ _YAM_ ARNDAL_ CENTR_ in letters that were roughly three-feet high. You could read them as you waited for the buses that drove past Denise's school. There may have been people in Little Atherton who had no personal knowledge of Denise Monton, who did not remember the name of the girl who had not died that day on top of the Rucks and did not know who she was, but there was no one in Little Atherton who did not know what she was.

IS A MURDERER was added, in waterproof felt tip, to her name on her locker, her school bag and books.

'Back your book again, please,' the teachers would tell her when they saw her exercise book.

'But it wasn't me that done it.'

'The book is your responsibility. It's your job to look after it, and anyway, quite frankly, Denise, you bring it all on yourself.'

Break was a misery. They called her the Antonym Bird again and squawked loudly in her ears and then burst out in hysterical laughter. She was kicked in crowded corridors by pupils she did not even know. Bruises covered her legs. She lay down and let the same thing happen to her neck one day in the toilets. The whole school had decided that Denise Monton was a legitimate target. She asked for it, they said. She irritated them with her whining ways and, if what she said was true, she deserved it. I ask for it and I deserve it, thought Denise, taking the knocks like a saint and consequently irritating everyone even more.

'Of course I always suspected,' said one woman to another. 'I think we always suspected something.'

'Be blind not to suspect something. You get a feeling when everything isn't quite right, don't you?'

'Well, I ask you. Two girls, right, up on those Rucks. They're fighting and one of them dies and it just so happens that this hole comes out of nowhere, right, and swallows one of them up. It swallows one of them up but not the other. One of them – magically – lives. Well, you know what I'm saying. And did you know that the mother is Welsh and what's she doing here if she's Welsh?'

'Ought to bugger off where they came from then. Ought to have done it long ago.'

The Montons were snubbed in the streets and neighbours turned away. Little Atherton sent the Montons to Coventry and Mrs Monton wished they really were in Coventry.

'No one talks to me any more and they won't let me use the drier in the laundrette. They say it's being used and I can see it's empty, I can see it.'

She wished they were anywhere but where they were, anywhere where women didn't push in front of her in the shops or where the girl at the counter didn't delay serving her even when there was no one else in the queue. Even Monton found himself drinking alone at the bar, and men he'd been to school with refused to play dominoes with him. He took to drinking his beer in cans and at home.

The newspaper boy always made sure that the newspaper was mangled by the letter-box and the newsagent's turned a deaf ear to complaints. The milkman left the milk standing in the sun and even the sterilised was sour. When asked what the hell he was playing at he refused ever to deliver milk there again. If they did not like it then they could lump it. The Montons lumped it. The telly repair man put a piece of rubber between two valves when he called to fix their television. When the television was turned on that evening the rubber melted and the stench drove them out of the house and lingered in the furniture, in their clothes and in their hair for over a week.

Notes were pushed through their door: 'PISS OFF MONTON AND TAKE YOUR DAUGHTER WITH YOU.' There was excreta too, just once, a small lump of it on the mat one morning, plaited and steaming like an oven-fresh loaf. Monton found it when he got up to go to work – he was a store manager in a chemical factory at the time, nice job, he liked it – and he called his wife and daughter down to inspect the gift. Denise knelt down and peered at it. Her mother appeared not to know what it was, seeing it lying there, out of context, as it were, but when the realisation broke through it did so with a kick and a punch that made her twirl dizzily into the kitchen and slump into the chair by the kitchen table. She rested her elbows on the cool blue formica top and her head in her hands. She wept. She was a woman who wept but here she surpassed herself. Incomprehension and a more than justified feeling that she was being persecuted raged in her head. For a chilling moment she wished her daughter dead. She wished that Denise and not Deborah had died up there on the Rucks. How much better she would have coped as the grieving mother. Charlie had taught her to be that – but this, this was beyond her.

Her husband dithered awkwardly beside her, patting her shoulder and turning over the toast on the grill, making believe that it was a normal day in a normal week and he was a normal man without a daughter who was touched in the head.

'We'll have to leave,' she said finally. 'I can't stand this another day.'

'I wish I'd never got up this morning,' he moaned, buttering his toast and ignoring his wife. 'What a thing to do. Who could've done it?'

'Someone who's sick,' Denise ventured from the hall where she stood guard over the stool as if otherwise it might run away. It was a mistake to speak. She should have said nothing.

'Sick, is it? You want to talk about sick, do you,

Denise?' asked her mother in a mock-sweet tone. Then her eyes flashed and she began yelling, 'Tell us about sick, Denise. Tell us what sick means. You're the sick one with your Deborah this and your Deborah that. The girl's dead and you won't let her be. It's you with your lies and your sick ways that have brought us to this. Talk about sick, Denise. You just talk away at it like you have done these three years. You see where your sick gets us.'

'Gwen,' said Monton.

'They'll be burning us in the street next.'

'Don't talk wet.'

'Wet, is it? And that thing on the mat out there? No, it's not wet. I can see them dragging us out of our home and burning us. November's only a week to go. We've got to go away. We've got to leave here. We're marked out. Oh God, why did you ever know Deborah Ridley? Why couldn't you have stayed in the house that day?'

'We can't go away, not just like that. There's work.'

'Work! I've never known you consider that so highly before. I thought that was just a word you learned watching me.'

'Gwen, if you want an argument you'll get one.'

'It's not an argument I want, I want to get away from here. Work! There's work other places.'

'What other places these days?'

'I don't know, other places, somewhere, anywhere where they don't know her,' she said, stabbing back a tear with her forefinger and using it to point at Denise.

In the end they decided to move.

A brick it was that did the trick. It came through an open window while Mrs Monton was washing the dishes, missing her, just, but bouncing off the cat's head, braining the poor beast, and wobbling drunkenly a few more inches across the floor.

Chapter Twelve

Moving Montons

So the Montons did a flit. Early morning, sky like steel,
they loaded up the rented van quietly and stealthily in
case the neighbours heard them. The three of them had
been up all night packing, so Mr and Mrs Monton
decided to steal a quick nap before the long drive to
London but Denise sneaked out to take a last look at the
place.

She couldn't remember being up so early before – if
she had it had not made any impression on her. She went
out that morning out of curiosity; she wanted to know
what a place looked like when you were leaving it, but

she hadn't really expected to see it look any different.

That morning, and at that hour, Little Atherton looked vague and impressionistic, the grey light of dawn smudging the sharp black edges of the houses and turning the world she saw into splashes and dots of muted colours that fell together, almost accidentally it seemed, into the shape of a tree, a house, a road. She heard an owl hoot – an owl in Little Atherton – and saw sparrows flippering headlong down the street in front of her. A black cat chased a newspaper and another ran round the corner with a battered fish in its mouth. Denise moved in wonderment. This light, that owl, these birds, those cats; if she had seen a leopard stalk a flamingo in someone's front garden she could not have been more pleased and enchanted.

Then, where else, but to the Rucks.

The silver-spoon grey sky curved around the contours of the Rucks. Charcoal-coloured, powerful and immense, how could they ever be called eyesores? If anything, it was the hunched and miserable town that lay cowering at their feet that stole and maimed their beauty; if anything, it was the Rucks that lent their dark beauty to the town, making it strange and serious and other. Without this light and without these Rucks Little Atherton was just another town, just another Northern town. The Rucks were no blight, they were the jewel in the crown. No, they were the crown itself.

She ran up along the edges of the Rucks and as she ran she fell, slipping on a slope full of bluebells, it being March and spring. She bumped her way down a yard or two, cushioned from the hard-grained slack by the soft grass. She lay back and looked up and noticed that there was dew on the bluebells, sticky translucent drops of it.

It must be dew, she reasoned, for it had not rained that night. Dew. Dawn. Owls. These were things she had never taken account of before. She had not known such things existed in Little Atherton. She had thought it as deprived of nature as it was deprived of much else. She laughed at her own ignorance.

'What an ace place. I never knew it was so ace.'

The crushed bluebells seeped their perfume into the air and, daringly, she tore a handful of them up out of the earth, the sap spilling onto her hands.

She felt changed, magicked into some strange land. She had found a joy that did not depend on anyone but herself. It made her feel large and magnificent and as though the world was a bright ball of colour for her to play with as she wished.

If she had stayed there that morning and refused to leave the place she would have changed everything. She would not have gone left of North nor, in time, would she have stayed in the North but moved to the right, perhaps, to the West where the sea is. She might have smashed the compass entirely and moved at will. But she did not stay. Her head humming with the song of the Rucks, she returned to her parents, whose faces were swollen from lack of sleep and excess of worry and who scolded her warmly and with the joy of taking their troubles out on the one responsible for them.

'You look like a dog's dinner. Where've you been?'

'Out.'

'Don't give us "out". She's been on them Rucks. You can see it on her socks.'

'So.'

'Don't "so" me, madam, or I'll give you a thick ear. Now get in the back of that van. And let's have no more lip or nonsense. We've had enough.'

Despite her sulky expression, Denise was radiant. She was, after all those years in the one spot, in love with Little Atherton. She tried to put a name to whatever it was that she was feeling but could not. She felt happy and strong and knew that whatever it was that so puffed up her soul and dizzied her mind, whatever it was she had witnessed up there on the Rucks, had the power to make a difference to her life.

She sat on the back seat of the van and hugged herself, she felt so precious. She felt like a bird with eggs in her nest. She had only to sit tight, keep warm and they would hatch. Birds of great and wonderful plumage would emerge full-grown with wings of blue and copper and on their backs she would fly away.

It was when the van started, when her father turned the key and the engine sounded, that it hit her, the obvious, the obvious hit her like a lead ball in the pit of her stomach – the realisation that she was leaving the place, that she would never, or not for years perhaps, see Little Atherton again.

Joy turned bitter, the beautiful thoughts curdled and those eggs dropped from the nest and were splattered on the hard ground.

The fine things that she had felt but could not name shivered and were gone, and all that was left was a name she knew only too well, an oh-so-familiar name, and that name was Deborah.

Deborah.

Who else?

What else?

Deborah.

Wasn't it just the sort of trick you'd expect her to play,

making you love a place just as you were going to leave it, making you want to stay when you really have to go.

Denise recognised the hand of Deborah in all of this. She was always the stirrer, the tease. What else could it be but Deborah's revenge?

Denise saw it all too clearly, saw Deborah in some white-walled Heaven sticking pins into a Denise doll. Deborah was out to foul up Denise's life because it is not sufficient to confess to a crime, you have to pay for it too. Deborah would make sure that Denise paid and paid high. Denise was certain of it. Denise wouldn't be able to do a thing about it. It was useless to get back at her because Deborah was beyond getting. Her revenge would always be total.

And whose fault was it that she was beyond getting and whose fault was it that she wanted revenge but hers, hers.

What right had she to complain?

Anger subsided, disappointment and fear fled. All three were useless. Awe replaced them. Denise felt herself to be as impressed by the prospect of a vengeful Deborah as she had been by the dawn.

Such power we give to the dead. Why, thought Denise as the van turned left onto the motorway, it can move Montons.

Part Two

LEFT

Chapter One

Life in the Smoke

In London life was easier, or so thought Mr Monton as he settled down, deep and comfortable, into the newish sofa for an after-dinner snooze that would last until the *News at Ten*. Big city life exhausted him more than life in Little Atherton had done, but it pleased him more as well. He'd found a job quite sharpish as a store manager for a firm of wallpaper manufacturers in Hackney. He worked nights mostly, and the money was sorely needed for London did not come cheap and he did not need his wife's complaints about the prices to tell him so because he could tell it from the bus fares and the price of a watery pint. Shocking it was, but when Mrs Monton got a job in the evenings charring in an office block nearby the family began to stand on its feet again. Shelter had provided them with a flat in Islington almost the day they arrived. Fortune had grinned on them ever since they had left Little Atherton. The flat, two bedrooms, a living room and a kitchen-cum-bathroom seven storeys up, was small, damp and dark but it suited their needs. True, his wife and daughter feared the long and threatening journey up and down in the foul-smelling lifts but the flat itself was a bolt hole.

Islington, Angel Islington, the Angel, the blue square on the Monopoly board, the one he'd always try to buy because the houses were so cheap and you could easily get a hotel and people were forever landing on it, the name thrilled him for it was near to poetry even if the place wasn't. He liked to say the word to himself. True, it was shabby and the neighbours mostly black, but they kept themselves to themselves and after Little Atherton that was a blessing. The only thing he didn't like was their music, which of an evening disturbed his rest and gave him a thin, fitful sleep. He couldn't remember hearing music in Little Atherton but perhaps London walls were thinner and radios louder.

Mrs Monton was less happy, but then for her contentment was a phantom thing as attainable as the Grail. A fated family history, a dead son, a touched daughter, vindictive neighbours, exile to a dirty city, a missed bus, a stew that cooked too long and spoiled, it was all water on her mill, it kept her going. She pursued each catastrophe, large or small, with hungry and magnifying eyes. She chewed the marrow from each bone of contention and sucked each problem of every last drop of significant misery. Life was a meal spoiled by mistaking the sugar for the salt and Mrs Monton ate it hungrily, complaining all the while. In short, she found as much to despair of in London as she could do anywhere.

In this Denise was fast becoming her mother's daughter, but it had to be said that although she was still fizzy with grief she was very much quieter.

'She seems to have settled down here all right,' said her father.

'Seems to have, yes.'

'Never mentions Deborah.'

'No, but that is not to say she doesn't think about her.'

'Thinking's no harm.'

'Well, you'd have to do some to know about it, wouldn't you? Anyway, I wouldn't count on it. Still, she's quieter. There's a blessing.'

It was true that Denise never mentioned Deborah, but she thought about her a great deal. She thought about Deborah as often as she breathed air.

Hate occupied her, too, for that was part of the curse her dead friend had laid upon her, the curse of falling in love with Little Atherton, a place from which she must now feel forever barred. It was this love that made London hateful to her. She hated the school to which she was now sent and which was so large that she was always lost in it, spending whole periods wandering up and down corridors looking for the right room. She hated the staff, who couldn't keep discipline and so struck bargains with louts. She hated the other girls. She thought their faces hard and their accents irritating. She hated their love of fashion and music with a beat, but not much else, and their soft, gooey expressions whenever they talked of boys, which was mostly. They were strong girls who could answer teachers back and teach navvies to swear, but they melted before any wimp they had chosen to adore. The boys were wet and crude, had faces splattered with acne and Clearasil cream. Their mouths were hard and mean, their lips cracked and their laughter raucous and cruel. Most of all she hated London, having to live in it, walk around in it. She hated its ugly squares of green, its tower blocks – the glass ones that reflected the sky and the grey ones that matched it – its busy thundering roads, the pace, the unfriendliness, the dirt. In short, she hated. It was a full-time activity. Denise was not a person rich and various in her moods. Both her intellect and her sensibility were narrow and crude – had they been otherwise her life and this story would have been entirely different. Her emotions, like her vocabulary, were limited. She felt deeply but uneconomically. Nor was she original in her hatreds, except in this: she hated coal; she hated the coal that came in blue polythene bags on the backs of lorries or lay like drunks on the pavement outside hardware shops. It wasn't real coal. It wasn't even like real coal or like the left-over coal, the slack that gathered into hills, giant heaps that gave forth bluebells, the Rucks.

But what of Deborah? How did she find London? What hole had she found to live and lie in? What hole else but the one in Denise's mind, the hole death had made. Deborah filled the vacuum that Nature had such a thing against.

When Denise was in primary school – sharing a desk with Deborah Ridley who had worn her hair in plaits then with a different ribbon each day – on one of the classroom walls there had been a picture that had fascinated her. In it a boy was kneeling by a river, and behind him, a soft expression on its face, was an angel in a long white smock and with sweeping pink wings. The picture was used to teach the children about guardian angels, to remind them of their constant presence.

'Tell the truth,' the teacher would say. 'Did you knock Amanda's paint over on purpose?'

'No, Miss, it were an accident.'

'Remember your guardian angel, Denise. You can't lie to him. He watches over you all the time. He knows when you're telling the truth. He's standing by your side right now just like in the picture. Is he shaking his head in shame, Denise?'

'I did it on purpose, Miss.'

Denise had had a crush on her guardian angel, had made good friends with him, had had long chats and played games with him. Now she no longer believed in such things, had grown bored with the whole business, but if ever she had been asked to describe how Deborah's presence made itself felt she would have compared it to that of her old guardian angel – 'She's there, watching me, standing by my side, has been all the time since we left Little Atherton.' Of course, no one did ask her, because at home the subject was taboo and her parents had begged her to be quiet at school.

People did wonder, however. They couldn't help but wonder at the red-headed, gawky girl who still wore her old school uniform at her new school and who never tried to make friends. She wasn't hostile to the other pupils, simply aloof. It did not take long for them to sense that something was wrong. They weren't sure – and no one could have guessed exactly – but they guessed that she was . . . what . . . tapped . . . a bit soft in the head? They would not have put it like that, of course, for those are Northern expressions and Denise was a long way from there.

Such was life in the big city, but Denise, hidden away in her bedroom, Dali posters on the wall, Radio 4 full blast, Denise moved to a different tune – one only she could hear. There was also Deborah to keep her company. Deborah, the crumpled golliwog at the bottom of a mineshaft, now lay crouched but cosy in the warmth of Denise's mind.

Chapter Two

The Needle

Looking at Denise's bedroom walls, the three Salvador Dali posters might have suggested a certain richness of mind. The posters were common enough, though not in the rooms of girls of Denise's type and background, but she had chosen them not because she liked them but because they shocked her mother. The pictures of roving eyeballs and of flies feasting on severed and elongated limbs made Denise's room an unpleasant and uninviting place for Mrs Monton. The posters helped guarantee privacy. There were no books other than school books and there were no records. The Montons had left their record player in Little Atherton and could not afford to have it replaced, but Denise would not have wanted it if they could. There was a transistor radio, a small one in a battered, red leather case, and this was permanently tuned into Radio 4, long wave. Pop stations irritated her whereas Radio 4 was mostly talk. She listened to the radio most evenings, but now with the volume low and barely on station except at odd times when she would turn it up so loud that the speaker would hum and crackle and spit with the effort. When not at school she was in her room, and when in her room she lay on the bed sleeping or staring about her as she listened with oddly rapt attention to the barely audible radio wearing itself down to a splutter.

Whatever it was that Denise heard on that radio it helped her cope with life in London. It kept her calm. Perhaps she should have lent the radio to her mother, for Mrs Monton found life difficult to deal with in London and was fast becoming a recluse, had been since the day a ten-year-old girl with a flick knife and a butterfly tattooed on her cheek had trapped her in the foul-smelling lift of their tower block and taken her week's wages.

'Hand it over, luv, or I'll slit you from cunt to tit.'

'I never knew that children could know such language,' said Mrs Monton afterwards. She dropped her cleaning job and insisted that she be allowed to retire early. She was not going to walk along those mean streets, mop those cruel floors or deal with those vicious Londoners any more. She resigned. She withdrew from life. Monton would have to look after, protect her.

'What else good is a husband if he doesn't keep his wife from working? Pretend I'm sick, pretend I've had a heart attack and the doctor has told you I am to do no more work. Do me that kindness if nothing else.'

Increasingly it was Denise who did the shopping, paid the rent, took the washing, ran the errands, so much so that weeks could and did pass without Mrs Monton leaving the flat. She'd sit in the kitchen with next door's cat for company and gaze out of the window at the city that had attacked and assaulted her. Life, which had always been menacing, was now openly aggressive. In the general threat that the world posed she came to see that there was one sanctuary and that was Wales. She became convinced that Wales was the one place in Britain where she and her family would ever be safe. She laboured to convince her husband and daughter that this was so.

'The air is clean in Wales, and bread, it's only tuppence and it's fresh. You'll never have tasted fresh bread, Denise, not fresh bread. The women wear pointy hats and white aprons and there's space there and good neighbours, too. Let's go there, the three of us. Let's pack up and go tomorrow. You can buy bread there for the price of a box of matches. Just think of the money we'd save.'

Monton ignored his wife's suggestions, for to listen to them would be to ask questions about her sanity, the answers to which he was too lazy to contemplate. Tactfully, he allowed his wife to serve notice on life and made Denise take over.

'Your mam's not well, our kid. Get your coat on and go to the shops for your mam, all right. Gwen, it's all right. You don't have to stir. Our Denise'll go for you.'

'She's suited to going. She's not known clean air and good people. And when you go, Denise, you look at the

85

price of bread and you tell your dad if I'm not telling the truth.'

The Montons drifted apart. Each member, so intent on cultivating his or her own eccentricities, had little time to worry over the others. They had never been a close family. Proximity had always produced conflict, dissatisfaction and irritability. Adversity separated rather than united them. The move to London and away from Little Atherton hadn't helped, but it had been a slow and definite process, this separation; it had been in motion since the death of Granda' Jones – back in the front room of the house in Little Atherton, hadn't he always seemed the still, whistling centre of them all? Perhaps, though, the process had begun with the death of Deborah Ridley or Charlie Monton or even Charlie's father. Had those poisonous currants led to this? Perhaps Mrs Monton had been right about God choosing her tribe to be the poor man's Kennedys. How many times does the axe need to bite into the tree for the tree to fall, particularly if the axe is feasting not on some sturdy oak but on a slender willow? At night Monton slept in front of the television set until close-down came with a long jarring buzz and the light from the foggy screen turned the dark room a soft blue. Mrs Monton sat in the kitchen stroking next door's cat, singing 'Marchog Jesu', or rather humming it for she had long since forgotten the words, and dreaming of green valleys, fresh bread and ladies in black dresses, white aprons and pointy hats. Denise kept to her room and listened to the snap, crackle and pop of the off-tuned radio.

Denise was not unhappy. Happiness did not enter into it. She drifted numbly, purposely drifted. The voice, the child's voice that slipped and weaved its way through the ragged pattern of the radio static, whose words had to be pieced together one by one, told her what to do, what to feel – and when that voice could not be heard there was always the voice in her head that could pass for thought, the voice that whispered, 'Let happen what happens.'

For Denise the voice was but another form of Deborah, one of the many, for it seemed as if the whole world was saturated by the dead girl. The Deborah who was the voice in her head was no different from the Deborah of her memory, the Deborah she heard through the static on the radio or the guardian angel who was never far from her side, never less than a foot away. Deborah was the voice that lived in the warmth of her mind and repeated the same message again and again, like a dusty needle stuck in a groove.

The needle was stuck in the groove, but that could be easily remedied. Somebody need only lift the needle. If she would not do it herself, then somebody else would do it for her.

Chapter Three

The Needle Comes Unstuck

Colin Saville could not have chosen a better day on which to meet Denise. It was a cold and feverishly bright February day, and perhaps it was the sunlight that made Denise feel slightly less Deborah-ridden than usual. Her good mood, however, was just about to disappear as she struggled out of the door of Lennon's supermarket with a shopping trolley and two heavy bags. Not only had she this weight to carry but, the bill having eaten into the money she had reserved for bus fare, she had a long way to carry it. She wouldn't have known what to do if Colin Saville had not chosen that moment to enter her life.

'Can I help you? You look as if you need it.'

She looked up and saw him standing close by, smiling down ̇ at her, ten years older than the sixteen-year-old Denise, with an olive skin that made him look foreign and romantic and a Northern accent to remind her of home. He was one stop away from Mills and Boon, and she was a blink away from love at first sight. He pointed proudly to a dusty blue Volkswagen – his chariot – and offered her a lift.

'That's dead good of you but I don't want to put you to any trouble. I don't live far. Not far in a car, but it's a long walk.'

'No trouble. Call it my good deed for the day, well, year more likely. The name is Colin. Colin Saville.'

'Denise. Denise Monton.'

So generous and chivalrous an act is rare in any city, especially London, and young girls anywhere would do well to be suspicious of such gallantry, but Denise was not. For so long she had repulsed every friendly move made towards her and yet that day she accepted a lift of a total stranger. Truth to tell, she would have accepted a lift from any total stranger and on the dullest of days because, of late, she and guardian angel Deborah, communing through the static on the battered transistor, had agreed that if Deborah wanted Denise on the other side of the radio, that is, on her side, then Deborah had only to arrange it and Denise would fall in with her plans. If Deborah wanted her garrotted and raped in a Fulham car park only the car and the man had to be provided and Denise would let herself be driven to her doom. So perhaps it was not so unusual that Denise accepted this offer of a lift from this perfect stranger, but that she fell in love with him for offering it was very much out of character.

She was safe enough, however, with Colin Saville. Colin simply liked to be spontaneous and considered vaguely eccentric. He saw a girl who needed help. He gave it. That was all. Colin was running a Volkswagen and the top half of a Hackney terraced house on a PhD grant and capital from the sale of his parents' home in Norfolk. He was researching into 'Ambition and Social Mobility in the Early Novels of Thomas Hardy' and methods of living as amply as near-poverty would allow. He was making little headway with Hardy, but as regards the latter he was one of those fortunate few who, as the joke goes, not only know how to make a silk purse out of a sow's ear but a couple of sheets and pillowcases too. His olive skin and Northern accent could obviously charm, but he was also slightly plump about the waist and, try as he might, couldn't train his thin black hair to cover his ever-widening bald spot. Poverty (of a very exclusive sort), baldness and weight problem aside, he was sensitive, likeable and had clear, expressive eyes. God had been generous and had given him many breaks.

God, Monton-hater though he was said to be, had not been exactly mean to Denise either. The carrot hair had deepened into a rich red and had grown into a careless halo around the thin white face, against which the wide black eyes and letter-box mouth stood out quite attractively. No beauty, true, but she was striking to anyone with an eye – and could Colin, with such an excess of gifts, be lacking in that?

So, after throwing her groceries carelessly into the back, she strapped herself into the passenger seat and he started the car. No sooner had the engine roared and the wheels moved a yard or so down the road than a searing

90

squash and crack came from underneath the car. Colin braked hard and they were thrown forward.

'Are you all right? What the hell was that?'

A ginger cat had found a fatal shady place under Colin's car. Colin stood on the pavement and looked down at the sad, squashed animal.

'It's a bit of a mess. What'll we do with it? We can't just leave it, can we?'

It was Denise's idea to tip her groceries out of one of the plastic bags. Passers-by stopped and became a small crowd, looking on in excited disgust as she picked up the burst corpse by the tail and dropped it into the bag.

'We'll stop somewhere and dump it, right?' she said as she laid it to rest on the back seat with her groceries.

With Colin shaking his head admiringly, they got into the car once more. He started the engine and shoved a tape of the charts into the cassette player.

'I love pop music, don't you? I like anything that's short and has a beat to it. It's amazing the hold pop music can have on you. Pop songs are the nursery rhymes of tomorrow, you know.'

He sang every song and knew all the words, and in between he talked about cats he had known, London, the absence of God, *Look Back in Anger*, Cabaret Voltaire and the politics of the football pools, winning Denise's heart as surely as she had won his when, without a trace of repugnance, she had lifted the pulped-up cat and dropped it into a Lennon's carrier bag.

He did not take her home, but to a bookshop in Dalston and then to a Turkish cafe in Stoke Newington where they ate bread that tasted of cinnamon and drank coffee as thick as soup from tiny cups. Then onto a play at the Roundhouse in which six characters kept on meeting outside a cathedral and pretended not to know each other even though they did – or did they? Denise fell asleep but Colin explained it to her afterwards.

She had fallen asleep with her head on his shoulder. She had felt so comfortable there. He smelt of peppermint. She wasn't really sure of him or whether he was good for her or not, but there was nothing in her head saying no. She couldn't see what he liked in her. She was so dim and he so quick and bright. He could speak German. She knew that Deborah would not approve but the iron in her soul was melting. It was difficult to care what Deborah felt.

Finally, he drove her home and she admitted that she did not like London. Colin said that he knew lots of people like that but that he just couldn't understand them.

'Sure, when it's hot and the buildings close in on top of you and there are too many cars on the road and too many people on the street, I can understand that. But people who don't like London on principle aren't happy anywhere.'

'That's not true.'

'Well, maybe not. But there are so many people who just aren't happy anywhere, who always think that there's some other place where their happiness will be assured.'

'Come off it, Colin. There are loads of pretty places.'

'You sound as if you have a place in mind.'

'Yeah, I have. It's called Little Atherton, where I come from, and where I'll go back to if I can. It's got owls and bluebells and large black hills that sweep up out of everywhere.'

'Sounds nice.'

'Yeah, it does. You can't say London's nice.'

He laughed and tried to prove her wrong. He pointed out how the sky never went black at night but was always a dark, glowing blue, and just to the right of them was the moon, a thin slice of it. Then there were the soft, orange phosphorescence of the street lights, strung together like bright beads along the roadway, and the car headlights, which threw hot, yellow beams onto the shimmering, oily-wet roads, the red tail-lights glowing away into the distance.

'Converted?'

'No, but I get your point,' she conceded as she got out of the car. 'That dead cat's still in the back. We forgot all about it.'

'I tell you what, we'll go to Hampstead Heath tomorrow. We'll have a grand burial service. You sing a hymn or two and I'll get some booze and we'll hold a wake. What do you say?'

'Sounds nice. It'll be fun.'

'Well, I'll see you tomorrow then. Yes?'

'Yes, tomorrow then.'

'I'll look forward to that.'

'I'll look forward to it as well.'

'Will you, Denise?'

'Yeah, I will. See you.'

'Bye.'

'Yeah, bye.'

'Bye then.'

'Yeah, bye.'

Chapter Four

Yet Another Hole

There was an argument when she came in that night.

'Where the hell have you been?' her father asked in a voice that made her mother cringe in her seat by the kitchen table. He stood in the middle of the poky kitchen in his vest and pyjama trousers, the smoke from the many Woodbines he and his wife had smoked in their distress casting a blue fog about the room.

'Out,' said Denise, shrugging her shoulders.

'We know you've been out, girl. We're not daft, not bloody daft. Where's out?'

'I met someone I know and we went to a film.'

'You go out to the shops for a few things and you waltz

back in after midnight leaving your mother and me in God knows what state.'

'I thought you'd be dead,' her mother wailed. 'I was expecting the police round any time now to say our Denise was stabbed and messed with and left for dead in an alley.'

'Who is this someone then, hey? Who?'

'Just a girl from school. She was upset because her cat had just been run over and I was trying to cheer her up so I said come to the pictures with us.'

'You mean you went to the pictures with all that shopping? Why didn't you drop it off here and tell your mother where you were going?'

'I didn't think.'

'But it was good of her, wasn't it,' put in her mother, 'helping out an upset friend like that? Not what you expect in London, a kindness like that. That's the Welsh in her coming out, that is.'

'Ah, well, she should have said.'

'I'm sorry, Dad.'

'Having a friend to help you in your bereavement,' said her mother, 'why, that's like snatching joy from misery, isn't it?'

In her room, Denise turned on the radio. Radio 4 had closed down by now and so she turned the dial and found Capital Radio. She fell asleep listening to Spandau Ballet.

She met Colin outside the flat at six. She told her parents that she was visiting her new friend.

'She's still very upset.'

'A bit much, carrying on like that over a cat,' Monton had commented, but neither he nor his wife had any reason to disbelieve her. They were glad that Denise seemed to be making friends again. They were glad of

95

any sign she gave of being normal.

'I've got a spade, a bottle of Pomagne and an old missal I found in an Oxfam shop this morning,' Colin told her as they drove to Hampstead.

'Have you got the cat, though?'

'Of course, except I've changed the Lennon's carrier bag for one from Harrods.'

'Oh, very smart.'

'Well, I thought, bury the poor sod in style, no expense.'

They chose a spot by an old oak tree.

'The tree will give him shade,' Colin told her, 'and the poor sod will have a magnificent view of London. Not that he'll appreciate it much.'

The soil was dry and packed with small stones and digging even a small hole was not easy. Colin wiped the sweat from his face with the back of his sleeve and mumbled something about not looking very impressive. Denise sat close by, watching adoringly as he stabbed at the unrelenting earth with his spade and the wind rippled over the plastic bag.

Eventually a satisfactory hole was achieved and in it Colin solemnly placed the cat. He directed Denise to Psalm 129 in the missal and made her read it over the grave. As she read it, stiltingly, a small crowd of joggers and dog-walkers gathered around her, the second time in two days a crowd had thus formed. They did not make her feel embarrassed, although she knew what Colin and she were doing was eccentric. Colin turned to the small crowd and suggested that they all sing a hymn and, half-heartedly at first but with increasing gusto, they sang 'Jerusalem' as Colin covered the cat with soil.

'Go in peace,' Colin told them and they smiled and walked away, except for two people, a man and a woman, smartly dressed.

'I thought it was you,' said the woman to Colin. 'I thought, who else could it be but Colin Saville.'

'Jacqueline,' said Colin, laughing in recognition and walking over to embrace her. Denise felt a cold wave of jealousy rush through her as she watched the well-groomed woman with the clear skin and glossy hair kiss Colin on the cheek.

'This is Wince,' said Jacqueline, pointing rather sharply at the man beside her, a man as neat as she was but whose face was weak and whose manner was dithery. 'So what are you doing here?'

Denise noticed that Jacqueline ignored her and that Colin had not bothered to introduce them. 'I've just done my first funeral,' he told Jacqueline. Denise noticed the 'I've'. 'And what are you doing here, Jacqueline?'

'Well, blame Wince. Wince adores nature. Also, and this is more to the point, it is one of the few places that he won't meet any of his friends and as far as his season ticket on the tube will take him. Wince is married.'

The last sentence was for Denise. It wasn't news to the others.

Jacqueline then said that adultery worked up a thirst and she needed a drink. Would Colin and his young friend like to join them? Colin said they would love a drink. Denise reminded him of the bottle of Pomagne he had bought, but Colin said that Wince would probably stand them a brandy.

In the pub, as Colin and Wince ordered the drinks, Jacqueline asked Denise how she had met Colin and Denise told her.

Jacqueline smiled good-naturedly. 'Yes, that sounds like Colin, running over a cat like that. He is one of the worst bloody drivers I know.'

Chapter Five

Slipping Out

When Denise first met Colin she was still at school. In fact, exams were only weeks away. The teachers had said that if she worked hard she would pass her CSEs, although they weren't optimistic about high grades in those subjects that demanded either imagination or originality of expression. She plodded, they said, thorough but dull.

Denise had indeed worked hard. What else was there to do at night but sit in her room and do her homework or read through her exercise book again and again? Homework had been a convenient excuse to turn her bedroom into a sanctuary, away from fussing mother, grumpy father, TV, the odd boy who dared to ask her out and the girls in her class who thought that anyone so remote and strange must be a lesbian and were wary of her in the showers. Her bedroom, neat and pink, with its Dali posters and ageing transistor radio, had been a place of refuge. There she would lie and think of Deborah, commune with her across the dark gap that separated life and death, dream of her, hear her voice, broken and low, in the hum and spit of the radio static.

Then along came Colin and exams and Deborah were forgotten. When she wasn't out with him in the car, a pub, a theatre or a park, then she was in her room thinking about him, writing his name and hers inside arrow-speared hearts on the back of her history book.

'Who's this Colin then?' her mother asked sharply, waving the history book in her face.

Denise snapped it off her. 'He's just a lad I know. You wouldn't know him.'

'Why? Isn't he fit to be known?'

'Leave off, Mam, just leave off.'

'I hope you've not been turned off your books by him. You got exams next week. You leave that school with nothing and nothing is what you'll get.'

'Exams don't get you jobs no more. You can have degrees and still have no job and half the folk in this place don't have no jobs either.'

'We measure ourselves by the neighbours now, do we? Nice kind of standards those are, aren't they? Why, there was a woman in the next block that was murdered by a fourteen-year-old boy just last week. Strangled her with her own tights. It was in the papers and she was no better than she ought to have been. Them's your neighbours. Are them your standards too, Denise?'

'All I meant was exams aren't important no more.'

'Exams is important. When I was a girl I dreamed of being a nurse, dreamed of it. I thought it would be a good job with your own uniform and a little respect, but then I met Charlie's father and I said who cares about being an SRN when you can be an MRS and have a gold ring too. Then he goes and he dies on me and then I lose his son and the only man that is left to me is him in there snoring in front of the telly. What use was an MRS to me in the end? I could have been a matron by now with a whole wing of wards and an apron with a gold watch on it. Your granda' always said I'd make a good nurse. You get on with your exams. You don't learn nothing from men except how to get on without them for they're always letting you down one way or another.'

But sometimes young girls can learn more from their boyfriends than they can at school, or so Colin had said. 'Not just about . . . well, you know, that, but about books and films and life and the way people think and feel. A sentimental education it's called.'

Denise saw school now as years of futile struggle to improve her spelling, her handwriting, her manners; years spent tryng to be popular with teachers and pupils alike and never succeeding and always being made to feel stupid and odd.

'We click, you and I, Denise. We click together like pieces, interlocking pieces in the jigsaw puzzle of life.'

The beautiful things he said thrilled her to the very bone.

Skipping school to meet him in the car park outside Lennon's and slipping back in through the door of the darkened flat at three a.m., Denise's sentimental education progressed. Dropping out of school altogether, going home only to sleep and change her clothes, her education progressed further. She read Pablo Neruda and knew who was the lead singer of Tears for Fears. School called Mr Monton and asked him where his daughter was and didn't she know that today was Geography CSE? Mr Monton called through the bedroom door and asked his daughter where she'd been and didn't she know what heartbreak she was causing her mother.

'Out. I've been out.'

'Out! With them waiting for you with a geography CSE?'

'Yeah, out. What's wrong with that?'

'Who is he?'

'Who's who?'

'Come on, who is he? She's been with some bloke. You can tell by her face. You can smell it on her.'

'It's London,' cried her weeping mother, 'it's a loose place. You have to be loose to live in it. That's what it is.'

'You've been nothing but trouble since —'

'Since when? Go on, say it. I'm listening.'

'We've had to move once already because of you. Do we have to move again to hide our shame?'

'Shame?'

'Yes, shame.'

'Shame? We've got a woman next door who's on the game, the man below is a drug-pusher and the kid down the hall has been put away for mugging an old woman. What shame have we got?'

'She's not been walking the streets, has she, Alan?'

'What else would keep her away half the night? Unless she's gone doolally over Deborah again. You've always been a funny bugger, Denise.'

'We should have gone to Cardiff or Newport or somewhere nice and respectable like that. Why does God pick this family to throw his dirt on?'

'Why don't you two leave me alone? I'm fucking sick of it, I am, honest, I am.'

'Mind your language.'

'Mind your own.'

'I'll have my belt off to you in a minute, you see if I don't.'

'You do and you'll never hear off me again.'

Summer came, a good one, bright, hot and long. The school had long since stopped calling and so did Monton. He simply bolted the door one night while she was out to teach her a lesson and, seeing that the door was bolted and thinking it was for good, hoping it was for good, Denise decided never to return.

A daughter run to the bad and away from home, one more item on the long list of misery and misfortune that made up the Monton family history. Mrs Monton, now daughterless and so forced to walk those alien, threatening streets to shop and pay the rent, took to stopping folk: like the Kennedys we are, she told them, or the Barlows off *Coronation Street*. Of course, as regards Denise, the father had been no use. A heavier hand from the start might have helped but you can't train a horse full-grown. Their marriage, long curdling, went sour. Monton slept more than ever and Mrs Monton sat in her kitchen and took to eating vast meals and long snacks until her waist thickened to the size of a car tyre and her eyes sank into her increasingly podgy face.

'Like the Kennedys we are,' she'd say through a mouthful of pizza. 'Or the Barlows off *Coronation Street*.'

Chapter Six

Real People

She had changed so much since February that she had difficulty in recognising herself. The girl who called herself Denise Monton and made her way on foot from Islington to Hackney the night her father locked her out of her home was not the same girl her parents, Deborah and Little Atherton had known. This was a girl who was finding out that she quite liked herself, a girl who could be her own best friend. Oh love, she thought, it's everything it's put up to be. Yes, the past had been hard and she had not made it any easier for herself. She had endured it as best she could, but now she had the pleasure of knowing that she had survived and that survival did not come empty-handed but enriched those who had achieved it.

When she had tried to open the door of the Islington flat, pressing hard against it, thinking it must be jammed, and then realised that it had been locked and bolted against her, that had been a wonderful moment. It had been liberating. It had severed the ties and cut the knots that had bound her to a stale, deathly life and set her free to follow a better one. She did not even have to go to Colin, she could have gone anywhere, done anything at that moment. There was nothing she could not do. A sleek yacht, its ropes freed from its moorings, moving smoothly, magnificently out of a dark harbour, she floated down the Balls Pond Road to Hackney.

For a slow-minded girl who avoided thought and complicated emotions, the freedom was immense and confusing but delightful too. The braid of emotions that knotted her up was a tight, delicious experience, novel and powerful. Real people feel like this, mixed-up and head overworking. This is what real people are like and I'm one, too. I can be a real person, too.

The walk through the dark city exhilarated her and the thought of attack – of strange men behind walls, in shop doorways and street corners looming up and grabbing at her – warmed her blood. It warmed her not because she liked the idea – not at all – but because she disliked it. In the old days, the Deborah days, yes, she would have been worried walking along unlit streets, but her death would have been no great damage, no great loss. She had had no great pride in herself, she had felt only indifference. Now, with Colin, pride had been returned. It was Colin's gift to her. She cherished herself because he cherished her.

I'm thinking, she laughed. I'm thinking big things here. Deep things. That was Colin too. He thought deep things. Thinking was another of his gifts. What a lucky girl she was.

Now she was his and she was off to his flat and they'd have sex and it would be good. Sex had been much talked of, but as yet they had never ventured further than an admittedly extensive grope. Buttons and zips had been undone but no clothing, and it always took place in the back of his car or in the dark of his flat on the sofa, but not, as yet, on the bed. The pair knew each other by touch but not by sight, and knew each other in the cognitive rather than the Biblical sense.

Once, in a launderette, she had heard a woman talking to her mother about her sex life and Denise had listened in. It was in the pre-Death-of-Deborah-days and she'd been curious about the whole thing and was piecing it together bit by bit because she knew her mother would make a hash of it if she was asked. She and Deborah used to sit on top of the Rucks and swap notes on how it was done.

'Of course, Gwen, it's all in-out with him,' the woman had told Mrs Monton, whispering through almost-clenched teeth as she pulled a sheet from the drier and folded it so briskly and sharply it looked as if it might snap apart in her hands. 'He puts his full weight on top and he jiggles it up and down. It's like the death shakes of a beached whale. Where's the pleasure in that? Still, I never could get steamed up about it. I let him do it when it's convenient, but I don't smile or nothing.'

Denise had not been sewn at the waist during her

adolescence and she knew that it could be a little more sophisticated than that, but the fantasies she had indulged in had borne a remarkable similarity to the experience of the woman in the launderette, and, like her, she had never smiled.

Denise smiled now as she stood outside the Hackney tenement, the top floor of which belonged to Colin. Her feet were hot from her long walk. The light was on in his flat.

One of the other tenants must have left the door on the latch; Denise had only pressed against it as she reached for the bell and it had swung open. She walked into the dingy hallway, the floor a shabby kaleidoscope of carpet cuttings, large, fat flies buzzing around the dim, naked bulb, and up the uncarpeted staircase. The hall and the landing gave a bad impression, Colin had said. The flats and the tenants were really quite smart. It was just felt that no one paid the rent for the hall and the landing and so they left it to ruin. She knocked quietly on his door and waited patiently.

He had been in the bath and he came to the door in his dressing gown, his hair lank, bald patch glistening and uncovered, skin no longer olive but puce from the hot water. He looked surprised to see her and said so.

'You'll still let us in though, won't you?'

'Yes, of course, come in.'

Denise slipped off her coat and threw it on the back of a chair. Colin's flat was furnished with large, shabby dark pieces of furniture picked up cheaply from flea-markets and lit by a series of lamps of old and new design placed at different levels about the room. The second-hand furniture gave the place a used but cosy feel and the lighting made for calm and intimacy.

Denise told him what had happened as he pottered around the flat in search of clean cups in which to put coffee. He was nervous and agitated.

'Can I stay here?' she asked him in a way that excluded the possibility of a refusal.

'I take it you mean tonight, or do you mean for good?' Colin called from the kitchen.

'For tonight I meant,' she said when he came in with the coffee.

'Yes,' he said softly, but added uncertainly, 'of course.'

She looked at him as he sat on the sofa opposite to her. His blue dressing gown had risen up to his thighs. His legs were slim like a girl's but covered with curly black hair, his knees were smooth, not knobbly or lumpy. She joined him on the sofa.

'I didn't think about it being for good. I came here because it was a place I could go, a place I wanted to go to.'

'I suppose it's inevitable,' said Colin, 'it's just so unexpected. I always take my time about things like this. Your parents?'

'Won't have me back, or leastways I don't want to go back. If I can stay then maybe I can find a job and maybe you'll help me find a place to live.'

'We'll see.'

'It's all right to stay here for the meantime?'

'Yes.'

She kissed him and, curiously, he blushed. 'I want to stay here, Colin. I want to stay here proper. You know what I mean?'

'Yes, proper. Properly. I know what you mean. I'm just not used to being rushed like this. Hamlet has nothing on me when it comes to making a decision.'

'Sorry.' Denise pouted, and then shoved his knee with her foot. 'Romeo. "Can I help you? Why, there is my car. Perhaps I can drop you off somewhere." '

'Denise, I am not the natural, practised lover my swaggering ways can sometimes suggest. I have been known, on some occasions and not infrequently, to lose all confidence with my clothes.'

Denise laughed.

'I can tell by the way you're looking at me that you don't understand what I'm saying. I am being serious, you know.'

'You don't have to be, you know. I am sixteen.'

'Yes and that's another thing, you're sixteen.'

'Sixteen is nothing these days. Anyway, you've never bothered about that in the past.'

'We never . . . we never went all the way. I could take that but —'

'This is the permissive society.'

'A permissive society isn't necessarily full of permissive individuals, just as a liberal society isn't necessarily full of liberals — and how can anyone call this a permissive society when sex between two strangers can be so full of doubts and insecurities and —'

'We're not strangers,' Denise cried.

'Comparatively we are. With me, desire has to have a stand-up fight with each of my inadequacies at each new encounter. Will I be approved of? Will we have to have a conversation in the morning? Shame about my body's proportions. Will she laugh or be polite when all is revealed? Oh, God, there's nothing for breakfast. Are my pants clean? Do I take my shirt or my trousers off first?'

'Well the last won't apply, will it?' she laughed, pointing at his robe. He's nervous, him, when it should be me. 'As to proportions, what does *she* have to compare them with? What does *she* care?'

'Then will she mind if she knows that the last person I . . . who . . . had . . . was in this bed . . . Christmas Day, was a man?'

The answer came quickly, without reflection. 'Not if he loves her, she won't.'

'He does.'

'Then we'll leave the questions until later and he's got to prove he does.'

'Be gentle with me,' he said as she pushed the robe away, and she laughed quietly and happily, believing he was joking.

Chapter Seven

As in Dancing, As in Life

In the single-bedded adolescent fantasies of Denise Monton sex had been conducted with unsmiling efficiency. Sheets did not wrap themselves around arms and legs, preventing movement, and knees, elbows and other parts of her body did not clash against those of her imaginary partner with bruising intimacy but slotted into place with a magical and numbing ease. At its best, it resembled swimming, her body like water, warm, softly resistant, yet easily susceptible to pressure. In the sweaty reality of Colin's bed it was more like drowning.

If love has its own language then Colin and Denise

grappled with it with the fervency and adeptness of
toddlers faced with a bowl of alphabet soup and no
spoon. The desire was there – somewhere. Their
embraces were passionate enough, even the one that bent
Colin's little finger back. Words of encouragement were
offered, but when they were whispered down Denise's
ear they made her ticklish and annoyingly gigglish. The
feelings that words cannot express, the feelings that only
body can communicate to body were full and sincere, but
both bodies lost fluency as frequently as they lost coordi-
nation. Denise was tense and understandably uncertain
as to what to do to please Colin. Colin, as he had threat-
ened, lost his confidence and his erection with his clothes.
The morning found them hot, frustrated and bewildered.

It was not the morning after that Denise had
envisaged. The sun did not stream through the curtains
onto Colin's round olive body, on whose shiny chest
rested Denise's head, a satisfied smile playing around the
corners of her mouth. Just as the night had been filled
with blusters and apologies, so the morning came to be
filled with cool discussion and explanations. They sat,
fully dressed, on either side of the sofa, sipping at their
coffee, nibbling at toast, shuddering occasionally as they
remembered the night's activities.

'It was a nightmare,' said Colin. 'I felt as if I were
stuffing a marshmallow into a piggy bank.'

'It was my fault,' said Denise, taking it for granted
that it was.

'No, no, not at all, it was mine, all mine, no. I did warn
you.'

'Is it because you're queer?'

Colin winced at the word. No, he wasn't. 'Horrible
word.'

She apologised.

'No, it's all right. After all, I said as much, didn't I? It's not always like this – most of the time, but not always – and I suppose I manage to act as if it's never like this. I've got this swagger about me I'm told, I exude confidence, but the truth is that I don't so much swagger as flop from side to side. You picked a bad one. You should pick someone who'll make it easy for you.'

'But I don't want no one else. And there was never any choice about it. I'm no good at choosing. I've never been good at that. I let things happen. I let you happen and I let last night happen. That's how I am. I don't know what I can do about that.'

There was a silence in which Denise pondered this. She saw the person she had become and did not like it. She remembered how young she was and how she really knew so little about anything except her family and Deborah. Last night she had said goobye to them. Last night she had chosen for herself, last night she had chosen Colin and now he seemed to be slipping away, she was losing him. But how to keep him, how to stick with him, attach herself to him? Colin was a safe, dry rooftop in a flooded world.

She sensed the way things were going. She could trace in it that familiar pattern: hope led always to disappointment; after laughter came the tears. She could even hear her mother say, 'Tears before bedtime', and knew that this was how Deborah worked – but she was damned if she was going to let Deborah win again. Not this time, not ever again. She had spent long enough in mourning. Deborah could go to the wall, and if Deborah would not go there quietly then Denise would push her there herself.

'Last night doesn't matter to me,' she found herself

saying. 'Not one bit, but you do. I won't let you go, not for nothing. Don't throw me out.'

'I won't throw you out.'

'Don't give me up.'

'I won't,' he snapped back. 'There's no question of that. I wouldn't do that. I don't want to do that.'

'I love you.'

'Yes, I know. I know you do.'

He leaned over, kissed her cheek, sat back and smiled. It was the kind of thing that Colin could do well, small, graceful, sincere. It filled her with such faith in him.

'Let me explain or, well, let me try.' He scratched his nose and looked down at his hands as if the words he was about to say were written for him on his nails. 'Basically, I can swing either way. It never mattered in the past. It was never a problem. I had two sides to me and no particular preference. I'd go with anyone who liked me. I'd go with anyone who flattered me. Jacqueline was my last girlfriend.'

'The girl on Hampstead Heath?'

'Yes, we go back a long way and she was between men. You know what she's like. She's a good friend and we decided to keep it just that. I couldn't blame her. You see, I never loved her.'

Denise picked up the implication; the problem lay in his loving her and that was a difficulty she could not help liking. She let him carry on.

'You see, when you're like me then you look for love in any place you can find it.'

'Am I one of them places then?'

'You're the best place I've ever been in. No, I mean it. I look at your face and I see you looking at me as if I were wonderful and as if your life depended on me. I'm not

113

and it doesn't, but it's so good to know that someone feels like that about me.'

'Then why was last night so awful?' Answer that, she prayed, answer that well and set me free of Deborah. As Colin paused to answer, she could feel the room grow cold with the presence of the dead girl, could feel her impatience, sense her waiting to lead her back home by the hand.

'Oh last night, last night. Last night was just awful. Last night I didn't recognise you. You came in here glowing and strong and I didn't know how to take it. It curled me up inside. Now I can see I was silly and cowardly and a cluck.'

'Then it'll be all right?'

'It'll be fine.'

'Because I'm no longer bossy and all that. I don't want to be anything you don't want me to be.'

'You see, it's like dancing. Someone has to lead. Nothing is equal in life and, right or wrong, I can't or won't be led. I'm not making a general rule, just talking about how it is with me. As in dancing, as in life, the man should lead. Well, this man and for this dance anyway. Do you understand?'

She did. Her smile said as much, that keen, adoring smile she would always have when she looked at him. As in dancing, as in life. There it was, an easy formula, one she could understand. She thought it beautiful and simple. She could treasure words like that. Her panic fled and so did Deborah. She could almost hear the rustle of Deborah's wings as they beat a retreat.

'We need patience, consideration and trust,' said Colin. 'We'll get through.'

For Denise, Colin's words would always feel like cool hands on a hot forehead, calming and restorative.

Chapter Eight

A Fresh Start

Denise deserved a break. She deserved Colin, or someone like him, after all those years spent with Deborah. During those years Deborah had been Denise's constant thought, her all, the very beat of her heart. Deborah had been the flame around which Denise, moth-like, had danced. Now it was the brightly glowing figure of Colin that fascinated her, and although Colin had the talent to make her happy, was without malevolence and showed her that the darting flame around which she danced was love itself, it was still the same flame, the same music, the same steps. As in dancing, as in life, only her partner had changed.

Colin and Deborah, to each in turn Denise had given up her life. It belonged to them to do with as they saw fit. Perhaps that is what being left of North means: throwing your life aside and to the wrong side. She threw it over to Deborah because she didn't want it and she now threw it over to Colin because without him it wasn't worth much anyway. And hadn't Colin insisted on this sacrifice – as in dancing, as in life?

Denise would fill a gap in his life, would be insurance against loneliness and security against those feelings of oddity and discomfort he felt whenever circumstances left him without companionship. Denise was not his ideal. He had not expected to fall in love with her. He had always believed that he could not fall for anyone whom he did not regard as his match or, better still, his superior in looks, intelligence and personality. For love to be true for him he had expected it to involve adoration and so, ironically, it had – except that he was the one to be adored. Denise looked on him as though he were a god and he could not but like it, could not help but act like one. He was flattered by her generosity and her trust in him. Her devotion had the effect of increasing his arrogance but also of making simple what would have been, for him, a difficult relationship. It mapped it out, gave it a series of identifiable signposts. With such signposts the way was more easily charted, he could manage it all so much better. It was also a challenge. Denise was his and freely given, and he must make his mark on her, show himself that she was his. He would do it gently and with affection and care – and Denise would let him.

Colin was a literate man and like many literate men he could not resist trying to educate the woman he loved, and Denise seemed to want it so. She was so convinced of his greatness and so desirous of deserving him that she would not rest until she had been moved a few rungs up the ladder to be nearer to him. Colin had read and seen *Pygmalion* and thought *My Fair Lady* the second best popular musical ever written – the first was *Guys and Dolls* – and so he felt he understood the dangers of making himself a Higgins to Denise's Eliza Doolittle. He began to educate her not only because that was what Denise most wanted, but also to share with her the things in life he most enjoyed. Denise, for her part, would have happily sat through the whole of Stockhausen if Stockhausen had met with Colin's approval and if, in so doing, she also gained it for herself.

'Lawrence is a must. Did you ever do him at school?'

'All we ever did was books about crime and broken homes and kids running away. We read loads like that. One was called *Spiggy*, one was called *Crums* and another one was called something else. Dead boring. Nothing about real life.'

'Lawrence is very real.'

'I'll try it then. What's it about?'

'Everything – men, women, nature, civilisation, death, love. . . .'

'Love? He's not like Mills and Boons is he 'cos I can't stand them.'

It took Colin three evenings to read her *Women in Love*. Denise would never have read it for herself.

'It's massive, look at the size of it.'

He abridged it for her as they sat on the sofa in front of the gas fire. Denise would curl herself up beside him on the sofa, listening attentively as he read, hearing the soft deep hum of his voice in his chest and admiring the

117

orange sheen the light of the gas fire shed on his features. In the midst of rabbits and moons and bowels and cores of being there emerged a story which she could follow, but one for which she had little sympathy. There were two men and two sisters and the two men loved the two sisters and each other. One couple got on really quite well and the other didn't. The two men wanted to get on really well but didn't really. One of the men died at the end because one of the sisters was really rotten to him. He died in the snow and the other man said he'd always remember him because life was empty without him, which was a bit unfair on his wife because it didn't make her feel very important.

'I don't know why it's called *Women in Love*. It's more about men in love, isn't it?'

Colin said that was probably a very perceptive remark and did she think she'd like to read it for herself.

'I liked the way you read it.'

He decided that short stories would make a better introduction. He gave her Lawrence's, of course. She struggled with but quite enjoyed them. Some she read and thought, so what?, and some were about miners and they reminded her of the Rucks and so she quite liked them. And one was about a woman who married for the second time and her first husband came back from the dead to claim her. The story reminded her of Deborah. Could Deborah do that? Reclaim her? Colin saw her crying, cuddled her and was proud.

'It shows you have sensitivity. I envy you. It's years since I cried over a book. Value it.'

Later, she told herself, she would tell Colin about Deborah. She did not dare tell him yet for fear he call her mad or morbid and throw her out, her constant and purely imagined dread. So Denise never mentioned Deborah and Colin remained ignorant. She gave him a potted autobiography. It didn't sound much of a life without mention of Deborah, but then *Anna Karenina* isn't much of a book if you take out every sentence with the name Anna in it. It sounded a dull life, but Colin had not expected her to have any other kind of life and was aware of no omission in the telling of it. Denise felt guilty – she was lying to him after all – but she knew it was for the best. Deborah meant bad luck. Deborah, the word 'Deborah', was the opposite of 'Open Sesame' or 'Abracadabra'. It shut things off, it made things disappear. Deborah was the Antonym Bird, a black, perverse and winged creature that loved to upset and reverse the order of things. There could be no nesting place for Deborah any longer, thought Denise, I have served my time, and so she kept silent, thought only of Colin and of how much he meant to her.

'I love you and I love you and it is an eternal wrenching . . .' Colin had read to her, a line from a poem by Ungaretti.

'Yes, it is, isn't it?'

Colin smiled.

Life with Colin was all the sweeter to Denise, all the more sentimental, all the more romantic, because of the lack of sweetness, of sentiment and of romance in the years before she met him. She felt as though a chain that had bound her to a prison wall had suddenly snapped, leaving her free to escape, and in her new freedom she found few echoes of the prison cell to remind her of it.

'You know,' said Colin once, 'you really ought to go back and see your parents once in a while.' Colin's parents were long dead and he had been an only child.

Having no family himself, he could not understand the ease with which Denise had given her own up. He did not press her, knowing that there was something more about them than she was willing to tell and trusting in her faith in him that she would one day tell him.

'I will one day,' she assured him. She sent them a postcard telling them she was fine and not to worry. 'Me mam'll worry anyway. That's what she's like. It's her hobby.'

Denise saw that one day she would go back but dreaded that day. She had begun a new life. She had successfully separated herself from her old ways, or rather Colin had. She was enjoying the transformation he was bringing about in her. When that transformation was complete, when she felt strong enough in her new life to resist the snares of her old one, then, and only then, would she contemplate returning there.

'I'll go back when I'm ready, when I know they can't do me harm.'

Colin found a part-time job in a gallery in Kensington and another in a bookshop on Charing Cross Road. He found one for Denise as an usherette in a cinema in Bloomsbury, and on their wages, the dole that both continued to claim and the seventy-five pounds Colin made on the sale of two poems to a Canadian literary magazine they lived very well. The sale of the poems, one of them about Denise, gave Colin the confidence to call himself a writer. He dropped his thesis on Hardy and began a novel, a piece of magic realism called *Dreams I Had Too Many*. He spent his evenings on this solid and intense piece of writing while Denise was out at work. He averaged a paragraph a day, turning over each word in each sentence like a Rubik Cube until the word fell into place and the right pattern was achieved.

'Hemingway said that you had to work all your life on writing sentences that were true, and he was right, but it's not just that, every word in that sentence must be true and every paragraph and every chapter. I feel a great affinity with Hemingway.'

Denise said that wasn't surprising because they were both writers weren't they?

Once a paragraph, short or long, was finished to his satisfaction Denise would type it up. Denise was not a typist and plodded along with two uncertain and dyslexic fingers. It could take her longer to type up one of these paragraphs than it did for Colin to create them. It was Colin's idea and he was ruthless – incorrect and untidy typing were rejected and Denise was forced to start again. He could have done it better and more quickly himself, he told her, but he wanted to show Denise how art was created, wanted to involve her in the mystery with which he had now involved himself.

'You just don't bang these things out.'

So Denise crashed her fingers on the typewriter keys with a blind dedication, enjoying the challenge, enjoying pleasing Colin and taking the mystery on trust.

'You're becoming a proper little literary wife, do you know that? Literary wives do that sort of thing, sorting out manuscripts.'

Literary wife. It seemed the apex of achievement.

'Did you know Dostoevsky married his secretary?'

No, she didn't, but was pleased for both Dostoevsky and his secretary and by the promise their example held for Colin and herself.

Chapter Nine

The Return Visit

Denise discovered for the first time – or so it felt – what it was like to be happy. The sneer disappeared from her lips and that hard grudging tone in her voice mellowed. Perhaps she had been happy before but she could not remember such a time. There had been the times when she had sat by Granda' Jones and had been lulled by the soft snap, crackle and pop of his breathing and had been content. There had been times, too, when Deborah had made her laugh till her sides ached, but that had been the living Deborah, that had been childish, girlish fun. With Colin, happiness was more consistent, more prolonged and more warming. You could say that she was as happy as Larry had been with Colin – Larry had been before Jacqueline and long, long before Denise. She felt herself growing clever and her mind expanding to embrace the new ideas, feelings and words that Colin had given her. Early on, he had made up a list of things for her to do, a reading list, a list of good music to listen to and a list of words to be learned and used in conversation. So keen a pupil was she and so good her progress, that Colin could soon edit these many lists into a simple formula for self-improvement.

1. No time wasting, i.e. no sitting around looking vacant. Be active – always!
2. When relaxing, listen to music – classical music. Work your way through my collection. Familiarise yourself with at least one record a week.
3. Memorise one poem a week – no limericks unless absolutely filthy. Try short lyrics. NB: Yeats is my favourite.
4. Tell me you love me at least once a day. No more, I'll grow big-headed.
5. Read at least one novel a fortnight. We've no telly so no excuses. I read 2.3 a week. Beat that!
6. Show me you love me once a day in some way or other. Surprise me!
7. Watch at least two foreign movies a month. The ones you see at work don't count.
8. Remind me to tell you I l__e you. Fill in the blanks.

The formula was made out like an old parchment and was stuck on the fridge door. Colin asked her to move it from there when some friends had called round, seen it and had commented on it. She put it inside the fridge by the egg shelf so that she could study it every morning while she made breakfast.

So Denise changed – almost completely – but that was what she wanted, what Colin wanted. She wanted to please him so that he would never turn against her or think her unworthy of him. She became a faint but discernible copy of him, and so complemented, flattered and pleased him. She was his geisha girl from deepest Lancashire.

One day, in a supermarket, Lennon's, where they had met, she saw a girl she had been in school with but had never liked. The girl was on the check-out and did not recognise her immediately. Denise, wearing an RAF boiler suit, a blue silk scarf and her hair tied back in a bun, was not the grumpy, awkward girl with the creepy eyes the girl on the till remembered.

'God, I didn't recognise you then. You look dead nice. You do, you look dead nice. It's Denise, isn't it? You were a queer bloody fish at school, you were. Mind you, you were never there towards the end of it. You met some fella. You haven't half changed.'

'Yes, you seem the same though.'

'Oh, get lost,' moaned the girl. 'I bleached me hair for sommat to do, but it's growing out and needs washing. It's filthy, look at it.'

'When's it due?'

'Oh, you noticed. Some people think it's just fat. Not for ages yet. It's my second.'

'Your second?'

'Yeah, I know, I live life to the full and never do a thing by half, not me. Don't I just. Work here all day,

124

collect the other one from me mum, stay in with him all night. First time I went out after having him I met this footballer. Gorgeous he was, right out of my league. Anyway, this is his. I said to him, "You scored an own goal here, love. What you going to do about it?" "Nothing," he says, and he was true to his bloody word. You look dead nice. Going with anyone, are you?'

'Sort of. I live with someone.'

'My sister does that. What's he do?'

'Well, I suppose he writes.'

'Well, he'll have money then but you watch out, OK. Seventeen pounds and sixty-three pence, please.'

Denise gave her the money. 'Nice to see you.'

'To see you nice, yeah. You look dead nice, dead different, you know what I mean? You be careful, all right.'

As she walked away thinking, that could have been me sitting there at that till if it hadn't have been for Colin. She felt she had passed a test, had qualified in her new life and that the change from what she had been to what she now was was complete and would be lasting.

'You're not becoming a snob, are you?' asked Colin when she told him about the girl on the till.

'No,' she said, and supposed it was something that Colin would not really understand. 'I'm going back to see me mam and dad, for a visit. I want to see how they're getting on. Show them I'm all right.'

'Will they remember you?'

Going back was strange, alien. She was aware of every step she took, aware of each one bringing her closer home. As she turned the corner of the road that led to the tower block she had to stop. In her day that road had been lined with terrace houses, scruffy, grubby buildings,

125

but she'd liked them for their gardens, front and back, not large, not always cared for, but privet-hedged and green. Now these houses were empty, the windows boarded up or smashed, the doors broken or gone completely, the walls peeling and sprayed with graffiti, the gardens ruined and strewn with rubble.

'What's happened?' she asked a passer-by, a West Indian woman as broad as a bus with a tooth-filled mouth that seemed even broader.

'Nothing happened, love, been like this for ages.'

'Where's everything gone?'

'God knows. These here houses is coming down. They's building new ones. Like them up there.' With a twist of her head she indicated the tower block where Denise's parents still lived, and the way she looked at that tower block reminded Denise of the way in which the women in Little Atherton had looked at the Rucks, hating them but knowing them to be their fate, resigning themselves to having to live next to what made their lives dark and ugly. 'Like them, just like them. They say they not going to build things like that again but these new ones no different. No, love, brick is a different colour, that's all.'

Denise walked on to the tower block, made to go into the lift, knew that it wouldn't be working, that it would stink and be dark, and so climbed up the stairs. She stood outside the door and smoothed out her dress before knocking. The dress was black, not expensive but it looked it. She'd borrowed it from Jacqueline, the only one of Colin's friends who did not intimidate her. She knocked again, heard movement inside the flat but no one came. She knocked again and then again. She knew her mother was in, could sense her behind the door.

'Mam? Mam, it's me.'

126

'Who is it?'

'Mam, it's me.'

'I'm not here. No one is here. We have no money. Go away.'

'Mam, it's Denise, open the door.'

She had expected to be welcomed with recriminations, tears and open arms. She had expected it to be bitter and resentful, but easy too. She had at least expected to see her mother, not talk to her through a door.

'Open the door, Mam, open it for God's sake.'

She heard the chain being slipped on, saw the door slowly open as far as the chain would let it, saw the shadow on her mother's head against the wall but not her face.

'Show me your card. I want to see your identification card. You have to by law.'

'I haven't got a card. I don't need one. Mam?'

'No card, no entry. There's a poster at the post office says that. Go away.'

'I haven't any card. Mam, it's me. It's Denise.'

The door was banged shut.

Is that it, she thought, do I go now? She turned towards the stairs. She was half grateful but hurt, too, surprised to find that those you reject can also reject you. But why hurt? Wasn't this what she had wanted? To have done with them?

As she turned for one last look she was surprised but not relieved to find that the door was now open, wide open, and the hallway empty. Yes, that was it. Trust her mother to make everything as difficult as she could. She wasn't about to let her only daughter go without the usual display. She was in there, waiting for her, rehearsing for the grand scene. With that peculiar grace

127

of the victim she had spent her life acquiring, Denise went into the flat.

The hallway smelt of cabbage water or cats and stale air. She closed the door behind her and the hallway became dark, darker even than she remembered it. Her mother was in the kitchen, her sighs clearly and intentionally audible. She was sitting at the kitchen table, slouched over it, and somehow you could tell that she sat for hours on end just so. On the table was an array of some twenty empty milk bottles, all unwashed, the film of stale milk and mould blurring their shape. In the sink dishes and pans formed a clumsy pyramid and dust and grease sheeted every surface in the room. Like the flat, her mother too had gone to seed, but Denise had expected that. Her grey sack of a dress was stretched over a vast bulk. Mottled flesh buckled and curved and heaved from her neck to her ankles. It shot from her drooping shoulders to become arms as thick as a wrestler's. Her bosom and belly had merged into one large, inflated cushion. Her mother looked enormous. She looked as if she had been out shoplifting and had pocketed a three-piece suite. She would not have thought her mother's skin could stretch that far, did not think that anyone's could, but her mother's skin looked far from stretched; it hung from her face in miserable bags and jowls and round her arms, legs and midriff in generous folds.

'You look well, Mother,' Denise lied. It was the wrong thing to say but, to her mother, there was never a right thing to say. Everything could be twisted and was. What had been a characteristic of a lazy and selfish mind was now almost instinctive.

'Mother, is it now?' she answered. 'Mother? It was

"Mam" at the door. It was "Mam" for seventeen years before that. Why "Mother" all of a sudden? "Mam" not posh enough for you these days, is it?'

'Mam?'

'Oh, "Mam" again. Honoured I am by that. Think it pleases me to hear you say that?'

'I wanted to see how you were. I wanted to show you I was all right.'

'Oh, how good you are, Denise. So kind.'

'I've got a nice job. In a cinema. I live in a lovely flat. You'd love it. There's a Welsh dresser in the kitchen.'

'Don't flatter me with your Welsh dressers. And your flats. Look at this one and ask yourself why we have this one, why we had to move down here and why you moved off again and left me to cope with it all by myself and none of it my doing. No, you don't impress me with your flat and your dressers. I know what you are. I worked that out years ago whenever you stayed away half the night. I know what you are. I know what you've become.'

'What? What have I become? Straight out. Say it.'

'I won't soil my lips with the word.'

'You've got a filthy mind. How can you say that?'

'I know. So don't you bother me with your lies about how you got that dress.'

'This dress? This one was borrowed from a friend.'

'No doubt "borrowed" is the posh word for it.'

Appalled, knowing that there was nothing she could do to unfix that idea from her mother's mind, she leaned back against the cooker, and then stepped back to see the grease mark it had made on her dress. From the hall came the sound of a key searching for a keyhole.

'It's your dad.'

129

Denise's heart lifted. Sanity. The key was still searching against the door.

'Drunk he is and it's not yet four.'

Denise laughed at the thought of her father drunk, but caught her mother's eyes. Her mother's face was round and grey, as bland as dough, but her eyes were as sharp as knives. There was nothing funny in it, they said, nothing funny in any of it, never was anyway.

'Why did you come back?' Her mother's voice came quick and low, spitting out the words, quicker still as the door opened and the sound of Monton's footsteps came closer. 'Why did you? Why did you go and leave me here with him? Why did you make us leave Little Atherton in the first place? Why would you never keep quiet? Why did you ever make friends with her? I see her sometimes in this room. She sits back and laughs and tells me what you do because she watches you even now. She tells me everything even when I don't want to hear no more. She was evil. She passed it on.'

'Well, look what the cat dragged in.' Her father's voice, not angry or dismissive, merry almost, boomed in the poky kitchen, so loud it seemed to dislodge the dust. His face was stretched by a wide grin. He looked hale and well. The years had not damaged him as they had done Mrs Monton.

'Dad.' Here, at last, was someone glad to see her, she thought, someone cheery and improved, not sad and failing, not bitter and twisted who would make her feel guilty, blame her for the past, for the sad history of the Montons. Not a hugging family, she would have liked to kiss him.

'You'd better go, Denise.'

'Dad?'

'You'd better go. You left once. You're better off out of it. I don't mean it nasty, you know that.'

'I just came for a visit, that's all, a visit to show you how I was.'

'Then make it a short one. As for how you look, you look smashing, you look great.'

From her place by the table Mrs Monton gave a short moan to the contrary and turned her face to the wall. Monton snorted and looked at her the way the West Indian woman had looked at the tower block, the way the women of Little Atherton had looked at the Rucks.

'Go on, Denise, out of it. Best not come back. For her sake, not mine, and your own.'

'Don't you be doing a thing for me,' came her mother's voice, weak and self-pitying. Mrs Monton did not turn to them as she spoke but rubbed her face against the wall, which was wet, dripping with condensation from the steam that came from the kettle that had reached the boil and begun to whistle. Sharp and irritating sound it came like the bell of the final round of a boxing match. It was an alarum to fight, fight harder, fight not just to win but to hurt and to maim. 'Don't you be doing a thing for me. Why start learning to play a new tune now. When have I ever been consulted or considered? My life, my life's a misery and I blame her. And she comes back here for a visit to see the harm she has done to me and to show off her ways and I know and she knows that I know what she has become.'

'Shut up,' said Monton quickly, callously, like a slap in the mouth, but Mrs Monton kept on while Denise gasped and wondered whether it had always been like this and then supposed it had.

'A whore. How else did she manage when she left?

What else would keep her away nights when she was here and wouldn't tell us why? Let her deny it, go on, deny it.'

Denise said nothing, felt nothing. She stood in that kitchen, the scene of so many fights, watched the hard, indifferent face of her father and the wretched, lumpy figure of her mother, and considered her guilt in bringing all this about and considered it total. One push, one dead girl, dead not quite by accident, could lead to this. The kettle whistled on.

'Well, if she is,' said her father, slowly, deliberately, leaning over the table, his face up close to Mrs Monton's, 'I know where she gets it from and we know it's not from me.'

Mrs Monton turned quickly, fear and horror enlivening the blank waste of her face. 'No,' she said quietly, almost mouthing the words, her head shaking from side to side, 'I never meant that. That was just something I said. I never meant that, you know I didn't.'

'You say that now.'

'No.' Her mother sobbed a sob that made her whole body tremble and seemed large enough to shake the room. She hid her face in her podgy hands and wept profusely, and as she wept she rose from her place by the wall and trudged slowly out, defeated.

Denise and Monton were now alone in the kitchen. The kettle boiled on, its whistle cutting through the thick, hot air. Monton lifted it off the heat. The whistle died and Mrs Monton could be heard crying in the other room.

'Here,' said Monton, offering her a handkerchief. Denise had not realised that she had been crying. 'I washed that hankie meself. She doesn't do nothing these days. I do all the washing. I cook, too, but only me own meals, not hers.'

'Do you?' He was on her side, she could tell. Perhaps the visit was not a failure if it could finally bring father and daughter close.

'Who'd have thought it, and she used to call me lazy. Want to know what that was all about, how I quietened her down like I did, do you? Why she left? It were shame. She calls you what she does when she's no better herself. Hid it better, mind.'

'You don't think I'm that, do you? It's a sick idea she's got.'

He came over to her, stood closer. 'Ay, calm down, you daft apeth. No need to get upset. I don't blame you. I've learned things are different up here. You get by as you get by and you don't throw stones at other people. It's not like up North. Have you never thought that you don't look like me?'

'You mean I don't have your good looks.'

'Oh, you're good-looking enough for sure these days, but not like me. You look like Granda'. Have you never thought?'

'No.' She knew then what was going to be said, and what was going to be said was permanent and damaging.

'No, I hadn't either. It were something she said once. In a row. It were just after you left. Denied ever since and often, often, but I got to thinking and I thought, spitting image of him you are, not like me at all.'

Heavy doors clanged shut in her head to prevent the thought from entering – but too late. Monton's hands were on her shoulders.

'Your mam says you're on the game but she's twisted. I know you're not, but I know you're no innocent, not any more. Who would be? Girl your age, fellas round you like flies round a jam pot I'll bet. I like jam, too, and it's a long time since I flew round a pot. Know what I mean? Go on, it'd be a laugh. Like I say, you don't look like me at all, not at all.'

Denise screamed but heard no sound, fell against the door frame as she pushed past him but felt no pain, ran through the hall and out the door and down the stairs but did not feel her feet touch the ground once.

'I'm not going back no more,' she kept saying as she ran down the stairs, across the battered gardens, past the street of ruined houses and down the crowded high street. 'I'm not going back no more, never, I'm not going back no more.'

Chapter Ten

4Eva2Geva

Back in the flat there was a book on one of Colin's shelves, thick as a brick, its spine splintered and cracked, its cover dog-eared and ripped, and it was this book that Denise picked up on her return. She sat in the big chair by the window, cradling the book against her cheek like a rag doll, murmuring the title of this book that he had yet to read to her over and over again. She sat there till dark, until the orange street lights flashed on and were reflected on the oily-wet roads, until she saw Colin, ambling up the street, look up and wave to her. She waved back at him as if she had been floating in the open sea for hours and at last someone had come to rescue her.

'Why are you sitting in the dark?' he asked her. Turning the light on, he saw that she had been crying, saw that her face was red and swollen with tears. 'What's the book?'

'It's called, *You Can't Go Home Again*.'

'That bad, was it?' he laughed. 'Tell me about it.'

She told him everything that had happened with one exception – the reference to Deborah her mother had made – but there was enough in her story for him to understand why she was so upset. He had his arms about her and he comforted her as she told him of her mother's sad decay, her spite and Monton's claim that he was not her father and then, choking on the words, his attempt to assault her.

'I don't believe him. I think it was his way at getting back at me. It was his revenge on me for all the things I've caused to happen. That makes sense, doesn't it?'

Colin told her not to cry, not to think any more of them. He said that families had unlawful ties on a person and it was right to break free of them if they were at all uncomfortable.

'Blood shouldn't make the ties, love should. Families can be groups of friends or just two people like you and me. Parents and brothers and sisters and cousins and aunts are just categories in sociology and if we don't fit in with those categories then we shouldn't feel bound or guilty. If we want out we should get out.'

'That's not what you said before. It was you what suggested I go back.'

'Well, I know better now, don't I? Maybe it was because I don't have one any more made me idealise it all. But if they don't want you, if you don't want them, if

136

they hurt you like that, then just cut the ties. You've done it once before. Do it again. You've still got me. I'm your family now.'

'You're so nice, so good to me.'

'Why should your father want revenge and your mother blame you like that? What happened that made them like that?'

'That's the way they are. They blame me and I haven't done nothing.'

'Anything,' he corrected her. 'You haven't done anything.'

If there ever had been a time to tell Colin of Deborah then this was it, but the occasion passed and her name was not mentioned. Denise remembered her mother's words – 'I see her sometimes in this room. She sits back and laughs and tells me what you do because she watches you even now' – and knew that it was all too dangerous. Never rest, never settle or the Antonym Bird will find a perch and build its nest. So Deborah remained a secret, but a secret has a way of slipping out, like a plant buried in darkness, it makes its way to the light.

Colin was good, he was nice, he was perfect. He was always patient and calm. He was as good as his word and he never said a word that would hurt her. He knew all the right things to say and to do that would make her love him more, and as far as Denise was concerned there was nothing he could say or do that would make her love him less. He was her family now, her all. There was nothing else she needed. Colin and Denise. Denise and Colin. Col and Den. Col+Den 4Eva2Geva.

Her life wasn't just Col+Den 4Eva2Geva. There was the cinema job, the flat, the typing of *Dreams I Had Too*

Many, the study lists that Colin drew up and there was the Gang.

The Gang was the circle of friends that had gathered around them. They were mostly Colin's friends, people he'd been at college with or met in the gallery or the bookshop, although Denise brought one or two people from the cinema. They were young, glossy folk on the fringes of the arts industry, aspiring painters working in advertising, secretaries in publishing houses, failed MAs, *Guardian* intellectuals and the like. One or two would climb a few rungs more in their chosen jobs, but for now all were high on being young, metropolitan, slightly ambitious and fashionably poor (their clothes came from Oxfam but their food was bought at restaurants and their shelves were lined with hardbacked books). Colin, by virtue of his quiet ways and portly good looks, was leader, although there was a silent and civilised battle for this post. Denise was a member, too. She was, after all, Colin's live-in-love and authentically working class. They came to her flat and ate her cooking and whoever she sat by talked to her, but they were there for Colin and each other's company and not for hers.

The quiet pace of life always accelerated when one or more of the Gang were there. Life then had an IQ of 133 and Denise could not compete. They were all older than she and miles brighter. She was aware of her age, her ignorance and her Northern accent. It sounded so broad. None of the girls in the Gang had accents, although some of the men had. She never quite worked that one out. She took the back seat in the doings of the Gang, but she noticed that although the girls talked dismissively of the men, even in front of them, it was the men who mattered in the Gang. They led the arguments, made up the schemes, set the plans in motion. As in dancing, as in life.

But it was the women in the Gang who frightened her most. Sitting with them they reminded her of the girls at school in London, the ones she had hated so much. There was only one who was pleasant to her and that was Jacqueline. She turned out to be an actress who did walk-ons at the National.

Jacqueline was the nearest Denise had come to having a best friend since Deborah but that wasn't really very near. Not only were they so unalike, but also each chose to devote her time to the man in her life, Denise to Colin and Jacqueline to a quick but long succession of married men and no-hopers. Colin was sufficient for Denise. If she ever felt the need for someone else it was only because she wanted to tell them about Colin's latest act of kindness.

Deborah would have been ideal for this, Deborah, the voice in her head, the voice that had guided and kept Denise company for so long but Deborah had been banished. Deborah, she had forced herself to believe, was no longer there – but she had left a hole, an empty space inside of Denise, and this was dangerous for if ever she should return she would find her spot still vacant, would slot back with ease.

Where had Deborah gone? Had she disappeared or was Mrs Monton telling the truth when she said that she shared her kitchen with a gossiping ghost who filled her empty head with lies and sick dreams about her absent daughter? Deborah would do that. It was her style. And what if she wanted Denise again?

Denise asked herself this question one evening at work, sitting at the back of the cinema looking out for smokers. She regretted the question almost immediately, regretted mentioning her name after so long a time, for that very evening she saw Deborah again.

She was coming home from work. It was late and she'd caught the last tube. The lift to the surface was out of order and so she had to climb the long, high spiral staircase. She was alone. She was humming to herself the theme of the movie she had just seen. What she saw as she climbed the stairs she barely saw. It was a blur of red and white of a second's duration. She blinked, shook herself and carried on. It came again, that blur of red and white, just disappearing out of sight behind the corner. She stopped, listened. There was nothing, she told herself, but that was hard to believe. She moved on but at each corner there was the same fleeting blur of red and white and at each sight of it she grew bolder and more determined to identify it, although half of her mind had already guessed what or who it was. She moved faster, trying to catch it, until right at the top the blur steadied, stayed for perhaps one second longer and revealed itself to be the very image of a round-faced, pigtailed Deborah in a red shawl and her mother's high-heel shoes. Denise looked straight at it but the thing did not seem to see her. It looked right through her as if she, Denise, were the ghost. It vanished in an instant, leaving a pale Denise, panting, shocked and tearful, clutching onto the handrail.

'Oh God,' she muttered. 'Oh God, oh God.' She looked below her, looked down into the deep circular pit made by the centre of the spiral stairs, and remembered another time, another such long, deep, circular hole. Go on, fill it. Throw yourself down. It's what she wants. You'll never rest. She'll never rest until you do. You know that.

'Colin!'

Yes, she would tell Colin. She would tell Colin all about it and he would understand. Her panic would disappear and with it Deborah. She would tell him about the past. She would reveal to him what had been for so long the tender, open wound in her life, let the clean air of his sympathy rush to it and in so doing, in telling him all, she would feel herself healing.

She rushed home, but Colin was not there. Nor was he there the next morning. Afternoon and early evening passed and a desperate Denise phoned each member of the Gang but each member knew nothing. Deborah's got him, a knife in the alley, slit from ear to ear, a cackle of laughter from Deborah, a death rattle from Colin, face down, spluttering in his own blood.

It was ten the next evening when Colin returned to an untidy flat, an anxious Denise and an atmosphere so thick with Deborah it was almost a fog. He looked pink and guilty but unharmed. He refused to say where he had been, tried to start several rows, emptied a bottle of wine, filled a bath, sat in it and sang along with Mahler No. I and told Denise that he was in love, but not with her.

'Who is it?'

He looked across at her, guilty and resentful, through the thinning strands of hair that had fallen over his eyes but said nothing.

She asked again, flipping through the filing cabinet of her memory to find any likely girl with whom he would betray her. 'Is it Amanda?' Amanda, the tall, flighty sort, Denise had never liked her.

He said nothing.

'Is it Amanda?'

'No,' he said almost proudly. 'It's Ahmed. It's been coming for some time, but yesterday we just looked at each other the way you do and it just clicked and that was it. Sorry.'

That was it. That was how Colin fell in love and who should know better than she? If it had been Amanda then she might have stayed around to fight it out, but Ahmed, who was he? She did not intend to find out. Ahmed smacked of Deborah, obvious and humiliating.

Colin tried to explain. He said something about finding love in whatever place you find it but she wasn't listening. His voice dissolved for her like an empty promise. The inside of her head felt as cold and as smooth as a mirror. Thought glided off its surface.

She took the whole thing calmly. She would have his admiration for that. She packed a bag, broke his Mahler No. 1 in two and left without a word. If she wept then she did it silently. It didn't show. The tears welled up and hurt her throat so that she couldn't swallow without pain. Outside the flat she allowed herself the pleasure of those tears, and she cried not simply because the happiness was gone from her life or because Colin no longer loved her – and he had loved her, of that she was convinced – but because Deborah was back.

She had been pushed from the warm hearth to stand in the cold draught of Deborah's revenge. She knew it and feared it. This time it would be worse. Denise had been unfaithful, she had run away, she had forgotten her, she had betrayed her. Deborah was not a forgiving ghost.

Chapter Eleven

Tumble Thump!

Life with Colin ended almost as abruptly as it had begun.

When she left that night she went to Jacqueline's. She went there because there was nowhere else that she could confidently go. It was the only place she could think of without having to think about it too much. Her mind was occupied by other things, things to do not with Colin and his infidelity but to do with Deborah and her own infidelity. As she made her way to Jacqueline's she remembered that other nocturnal journey across the city the night she left her parents, but she remembered it now not as a journey towards Colin but away from Deborah, a journey she was foolish to have taken.

Jacqueline was indeed friendly towards Denise and there was not a twinge of hesitation or rejection in her welcome. She'd always felt sorry for the girl, and although her true allegiance was to Colin her own relationship with him had ended in a markedly similar way. She was more than prepared to hear Denise's tale of woe, but Denise was not particularly woeful.

'I'll only be here for a bit, until I find a place. You'll hardly know I'm here.'

It was hard to know that she was there, Jacqueline whispered over the phone to friends eager to hear the news. None were surprised. Few ever understood what Colin could see in 'Little Miss Gracie Fields' as they called her.

'She doesn't say much. She's out a great deal of the day looking for a place to live and when she is here she's practically silent and invisible. She's borrowed my little radio and sits in the spare room with it. The volume's down so low it sounds like two mice copulating. It's all quite morbid. Yes, Colin is a love, he really is, but you wouldn't become a nun if he left you, would you?'

Denise found a room – positively dull place, said Jacqueline – but there was some problem as to when she could move in. 'Of course you can stay,' Jacqueline told her. 'Truth to tell, I'm glad of the company.'

Somehow the news worked back to Colin. It didn't have to work too hard to get there – the way is greased by helpful others whenever the news is bad – and he turned up at Jacqueline's flat.

'I was all set for a big scene, tears and forgiveness, all that. There was none of it, none of it from her anyway.

144

Colin was distraught. He stood there panting and unshaven and she stood there without so much as an expression on her face. I thought, good on you, you know. I thought she was doing it deliberately. Serves him right, I thought. I only wish I'd been that calm, but now I know she didn't care one bit. He said he was sorry many times, many, many times, and asked for forgiveness, pleaded for it. He said the business with Ahmed was all over. He said it was an aberration and that it was she who really mattered. She didn't react at all. She stood there, her legs apart, her hands deep in this ugly orange cardigan she had dragged up from somewhere that was too small for her. And she did not say a word, not one. She stared at him as if she were bored with the whole thing and were waiting for him to go. So he did, but he was obviously upset. I remember thinking, Poor Colin, still wanting jam on both sides of his bread even when it gets too messy to eat, and that's when it must have happened. Three minutes later and he was dead.'

Tumble thump.

Chapter Twelve

One More Hole

Wasn't that just like life? Things go on all at a level, something happens, a hole, life drops through it and then it carries on – but changed. Tumble thump! Deborah was Denise's best friend, a hole came along, she fell in, life changed. Colin came, Deborah made a hole for him, he fell in, life changed again. Tumble thump! But did he have to die?

Suicide was how it looked. Consider: a distraught young man forsakes his live-in-love for a piece of Turkish Delight, repents, returns, is spurned, runs out of the door, headlong down the stairs and into the busy street.

He pauses impatiently at the kerb, sees the lorry heading his way and thinks, bugger it, why not?

Jacqueline was shocked and angry at the suggestion. No, that was not Colin's way. He had too much imagination to kill himself, too much intelligence and personal vanity to do it in so imperfect and messy a way.

'Yes, he was emotional, but that made him careless, not suicidal. He didn't look where he was going, didn't see the damn thing coming, didn't stop to think, that's all. He was a bugger with traffic, he really was.' Jacqueline looked to Denise for confirmation. Denise just nodded.

When Colin left, the door slamming behind him, Jacqueline tried to rid the room of an embarrassed silence by saying the first thing that came into her head – about Colin being a love and about bread with jam on it. It was she who found the silence embarrassing. Denise seemed not to notice. It was as if she had already forgotten Colin had ever been there. Then there came the sound of screeching brakes. Jacqueline moved to the window, simply curious, and saw the lorry. She could not see Colin, who was wrapped round the front wheel, but had known with an icy, instantaneous knowledge that he was there. She rushed out, shouting at Denise to phone for an ambulance. By the time she reached Colin he was dead.

A small crowd had gathered round the disaster and the lorry driver was sitting on the kerb being sick in the gutter. Jacqueline knelt by Colin's side. His stomach had burst out of his white shirt, now pink from the spread of gut and gore, his face was peppered by gravel, but otherwise he was unmarked.

A stunned, bleached-faced Denise appeared, gently

edging her way through the crowd, clutching a Lennon's carrier bag. She stared blankly at the body in Jacqueline's arms and in a thin, throaty voice began to sing 'Jerusalem'.

The doctor gave her sedatives. She floated under a smooth darkness for two days after and whenever she did wake, rising slowly through that smooth darkness, surfacing without a ripple, it was to the low murmurings of Jacqueline and the Gang in the next room as they sorted out the funeral arrangements.

None of them knew where to start.

'No one teaches you how to do all this. I suppose you're supposed to pick it up at other people's funerals. Well, I've only ever been to two, one when I was six and that I don't remember and the other was Marc Bolan's. I was in the sixth form and we took the day off. We stood outside singing 'Ride a White Swan' and waving our scarves over our heads and feeling very miserable. It was quite jolly really.'

Colin had no family, which probably made his life easier, but which complicated his death for those he left behind. Jacqueline took over. From the moment of his death Jacqueline became the expert on Colin's life and wishes, but everything that she did she claimed to do in Denise's name – 'Denise wants . . . Denise, I'm sure, would like . . .'. Jacqueline treated Denise as if she were the widow and herself an executrix appointed by Colin before his death. Denise made it obvious that she could not care less, would have walked off that very day if it had not been for the force of Jacqueline's personality and her zeal for arrangements. Colin was going to go out well, Jacqueline declared.

The morning itself was odd, very bright after a night of

rain. They met at Colin's flat, where the body lay in its coffin. They were all the same age, all friends and all felt varying degrees of grief but the same amount of awkwardness. They felt too young for funerals. The people there were more used to gathering for parties than burials. When Jacqueline decided to play a John Lennon LP – 'We need some music and this seems appropriate' – one girl almost got up to dance but Colin's coffin took up the space and the sight of it brought her to her senses. They avoided looking at the body, their eyes skirting the padded lining of the coffin whenever they were forced to look in it. Denise did not look at all. She sat quietly in a hard-backed chair, tracing the pattern of the carpet with her foot.

Outside a car honked its horn.

'That'll be them now,' said Jacqueline, heading towards the window to check. The hearse was parked outside – a white Ford Escort van in sore need of a wash and some rust-proofing. She knew then she had made a mistake and that others would follow.

Her mistake had been, when looking for 'Funeral Services' in the Yellow Pages, to pick up the *Evening Standard* instead. There, in the small ads, she had seen the name 'Morpheus' and the words 'reasonable rates' and had decided that her search was over.

She waved at the driver to come up.

The driver was a small man, practically a dwarf, with a cheery face so red it looked as if he'd boiled it before coming. He wore black, but the jacket and the trousers were of different shades and although his tie was black the colour served only to emphasise the pattern of Playboy Bunnies stitched on it in gold thread. He apologised because his mate who was supposed to help him out had 'flu, and then he clapped his hands together and asked for volunteers to help carry the thing down.

'It'll be a squeeze with them stairs,' he added. Denise noted the accent, a Northern one like her own, very like her own.

Five of the men offered to help, but none of them enthusiastically. Jacqueline was so grateful she tried not to notice how unequal they were in height. It was Denise who observed that they would have to nail down the lid before they moved it.

The driver slapped his pockets. 'Oh, no nails,' he said brightly. 'Anyone any Sellotape?'

The coffin, sealed with strips of Sellotape, was finally manoeuvred inexpertly down the stairs, the body bumping noisily inside it.

In the street they met another problem. Denise sat on the kerb while this was solved and Jacqueline, in despair, eventually joined her there. The van was too small for the coffin, or, as the driver liked to put it, the coffin was too large for the van.

'He was a tall sod, wasn't he?'

'Not especially,' sniffed one of his helpers.

They decided to budge the coffin up so that it rested on top of the passenger seat and was at an angle inside the van.

'You two girls will want to ride with me, I expect. It'll be a squeeze but what the heck, we'll be friends when it's all over.'

The driver wasn't sure of the way to the church and Jacqueline, her head wedged between the coffin and the car door, found it difficult to give directions and contain her temper at the same time.

'Here we are,' announced the driver as they finally

pulled up. 'I'll stay out here. I'm not fond of funeral services, you know.'

'We should have been here half an hour ago.'

'Oh dear, late for his own funeral.'

The service was simple, which no one minded. Denise just wanted it to end so that she could go away and have done with Colin, and the others, put off by the poor start, the cheery undertaker, the grim occasion, just wanted it to end. Jacqueline cried. She cried for Colin's soul and the mess she had made of his funeral.

'Is it over then? They don't hang about, do they?' said the driver, and immediately set about ordering them how to put the coffin back in. 'Now we did a lovely job last time so let's try it again.'

The driver drove to the wrong cemetery.

'We don't want St John's, we want the public one.'

'Oh, sorry,' said the driver.

Jacqueline, horrified, watched him put his foot down and set off for the right cemetery at such a speed that most off the mourners lost the trail.

The van arrived at the right cemetery long before the other cars. There was time for a fag, decided the driver. Did they mind?

'This is awful,' said Jacqueline. 'I wanted it to be so good for Colin. He deserved it. Can you forgive me, Denise?'

'Me? What have I to forgive?'

'Denise?' asked the driver. 'It is Denise, isn't it? Where do you come from?'

'Up north. Little Atherton. Have you heard of it?'

'Heard of it? I were born there. It is Denise Monton, isn't it? Our Dawn went to school with you.'

'Dawn Cole?'

'Yeah, our Dawn. I'm Craig Cole. I've been up here three years. Came up looking for work.'

'As an undertaker?'

'No, this is a sideline. I'm a TV engineer. I fix tellies. This is my van. I have two signs that clip on over these side windows here, Cole TV Repairs. I'm me own man. 'Course I take the signs off for this sort of thing and, hey presto, I've an hearse. Good, eh?'

'Apart from the colour.'

'Yeah, well, it's been commented on. I'll respray it. The cost of this job will cover it.'

'This job won't,' said Jacqueline. 'After the balls-up you've made here I'm not giving you a penny.'

'Now, hang on, love, a few hitches—'

'A few hitches!'

'Yeah, a few!'

'Don't give me that. You've messed up all along the line and if you think—'

'Leave it, Jacqueline. It's not worth the fight. Let's just get on with it.'

Jacqueline looked across at her. 'I don't understand you. You watch this man making a mockery of Colin's funeral and you don't care.'

'It's just a body in a box, that's all. Face it. There ought to be better ways of dealing with the dead.'

'Well maybe you might have been happier if we'd left him by the bin. At least he'd have kept his dignity. Look, I never thought I'd say this,' said Jacqueline, though her voice betrayed a cold joy in doing so, 'but have you thought how you might be responsible for Colin's death? Does that thought mean anything to you?'

Such a thought meant nothing to Denise. She was not responsible. It was Deborah. Deborah had made a hole and Colin had fallen into it. She had killed off Colin so that Denise would have no exit, no one but her to turn to. That was the way she worked, the way she wanted things, the way she was. No, she felt no guilt. It was all Deborah's doing. It was the way it was.

'You're a cold fish, aren't you? You're not the poor weak little thing we all thought you were. "Little Miss Gracie Fields"!' Jacqueline had found her stride, was enjoying herself. 'You're not quite right, are you? You're not all there, as they say. . . .'

'You're tapped, you're not quite right in the head . . . .' – that was what Deborah had said and then Denise had pushed her and a hole had occurred.

Jacqueline saw Denise's hands raised towards her. 'Don't you touch me, you cold-hearted little bitch. What the hell is he doing now?'

The driver had the van door open and was trying to unload the coffin on his own. His grip slipped and the coffin slid with a bang to the ground.

'You stupid idiot, why can't you wait?'

'I was trying to help. Doesn't look as if your mates are coming.'

'They'll be here.'

The driver turned to Denise. 'Our Dawn's married now. How you getting on?'

'Not bad, all right, you know. I miss home.'

'What, Little Atherton? I don't.'

'Is it changed?'

'Would it ever?'

'Are the Rucks still up?'

'Can you see Little Atherton without the Rucks? Weren't you with that girl what died up there? Deborah Somebody-or-other?'

'Deborah Ridley.'

'Yeah, there was a lot of talk about that.'

'It was all true.'

'There's someone coming. I think it's Mike and . . . Ahmed. I don't suppose you'll mind seeing Ahmed. You don't seem to mind anything else.'

Mike, an old friend from college, and Ahmed, a tiny doll of a man so thin he looked like six o'clock, emerged from a yellow van. Ahmed was embarrassed at meeting Denise. Denise took his minute hand and shook it, smiling politely.

'Let's get it over with,' said the driver.

No other mourners arrived after Mike and Ahmed and so they, Denise, Jacqueline and the driver carried the coffin into the cemetery. The plot – Jacqueline had a map – was on the far side. The coffin was heavy and the corpse inside it banged against the sides at each of the many jerks and jostles it received.

When they reached the plot they found it surrounded by litter, an old pram, dead flowers and a feast of bright purple weeds. A passer-by, an old man walking his dog, a labrador with cataracts, delivered the final blow to the party as his dog relieved himself amongst the weeds.

'You're out of luck, darlings. There's a strike on with the diggers. Criminal, isn't it? You can't even bury your dead.'

The old man pointed to a shed in the far corner of the cemetery and said that there were shovels in there. They'd have to break in, but they couldn't leave the dead out in the open air. It was either break the strike, break into the shed and bury him themselves, or take the coffin back home with them. They had no choice. The old man offered to help but Jacqueline said thank you, no, they would do it themselves.

154

They broke into the shed and stole the shovels, lowered the coffin into the hole and began to cover it with soil. The rains came and the soil turned to mud.

The driver drove Jacqueline and Denise home, where Denise's things were packed and she was ready to go.

'Before you go,' said Jacqueline, 'I want to apologise. Everything was going wrong and I was angry and I took it out on you. I didn't mean the things I said. I was a bitch and I'm sorry. I don't suppose we'll see each other now, will we? Well, I'll just say that I hope that things turn out well for you and not to mope and mourn. Colin would not have wanted that. Colin would not have wanted you living in the shades.'

'Thank you,' said Denise, 'but I need no advice. I know how to keep faith with the dead.'

Part Three

LEFT OF NORTH

Chapter One

Descent to Zero

Denise had snatched a little joy from misery and Deborah had snatched it right back.

Joy – she had thought so little of it. She told herself how she had known only three moments of it: the first when she had fallen in love with a dawn-bright Little Atherton; the second the day she had met Colin and that late-night ride in his car through the city when she had realised that it was possible to live successfully outside the North and yet not be left of it; and the third – its short life and its abrupt end giving the lie to time, giving it the status and duration of a moment – the time spent with Colin in the Hackney tenament.

Three moments of joy, a morbid girl.

There was at least one more moment that Denise did not dare to count. That was the moment of sheer, unalloyed, invigorating ecstasy when her hands had reached out and shoved best friend Deborah and the Rucks had opened wide beneath them. It was that moment, the one she dared not include, for which she was paying. That moment had a price attached to it and Deborah had returned for the final instalment.

The morbid counting of moments of joy was done to prove a point. It was a point her mother had spent her life proving. The point was that life disappointed you at every turn. Life was unreliable. Life was the enemy. It was the perpetual knocking of the cup from the hand. No sooner did the world convince the Montons that it and they were fine and that the heady wine of life's riches was there to drink than a heavy hand was brought to bear on theirs. The wine was spilt, it slopped out in all directions and became nothing more than a messy stain on the carpet.

Mrs Monton blamed God for such a mess. Denise blamed Deborah.

Abstinence was the solution. If Deborah ever made the wine flow Denise's way again Denise would not be tempted. Denise would see the trick.

From now on – and the idea had been there before but never with such strength and persistence – she would refuse to exist. Her efforts would be devoted to attaining zero.

Zero. Nil. Nothing. Nought. A hole down which she could disappear.

She would be invisible. She made a vow of it. She would hide herself from the world. She would be unheard. She would speak to no one unless they spoke to her and then she would spend her words like a miser. She would look at no one. She would stare past them into space if they approached.

Comfort was a thing to be avoided. Food and drink would be a mere suggestion, the barest outline of a necessity.

If people thought her a mute, an idiot, a bit touched in the head, that was all well and to the good. It would make the risk of contact that much smaller. Other people were inimical to being zero.

It was a penance, a double penance for a double sin: the sin of forgetting Deborah and the sin of killing her in the first place. Denise's idea was that by making her existence as minimal an event as possible she would make recompense for ridding the world of Deborah.

'From now on I'm going to be nothing to no one, not even me.'

Of course it wasn't rational. She did not think it out step by step. That was not Denise's way. Deborah, in her head, that little voice, told it to her and she obeyed. It was an instinctive response to her troubles. It was senseless but made sense, which was all she asked of it. She did not need reasons. The mind need not explain itself to itself. Only other people needed explanations and other people did not matter any more.

So it was a penance, but not one paid to God, one paid to Deborah. Who else would want it – or have need of it?

She settled down to her new life, her non-life. She had taken a room in Stoke Newington and a job, dish-washing for a canteen. With Deborah singing requiems in her ear, Denise went in mourning for her past.

Chapter Two

Tickling an Octopus

Denise worked all the hours God sent and her union allowed. The chances of overtime were good and so was the money, although, of course, she didn't do it for that. She lived on practically nothing and burnt whatever money she didn't spend. Working was something that cut down the time and filled up life. Working, it was easier to become zero. The mind was concentrated.

She worked in the kitchens of a bus depot in Seven Sisters. She was part of a team, the members of which were supposed to swap duties every day: Day One, on the till; Day Two, pouring the tea and serving the customers; Day Three, cooking the meals; Day Four, sandwich making; Day Five, stock-taking and ordering; Day Six, dish-washing. Every day was Day Six for Denise. She refused to swap duties. From the first day she had known it was the job she needed, the one best-suited to her task. Every other duty involved people. She spent each working day pushing a trolley between rows of tables, collecting cups and eggy plates and wheeling it into the kitchen where, stooped and blankly staring at the mildewed wall, she washed each cracked green cup, each thick, greasy plate, each plastic knife, fork, spoon and teaspoon with loving and religious attention, in water so hot and detergent so harsh that her hands turned a tender red and began to crack and peel.

The other girls in the canteen, four on any one shift, couldn't understand her but were glad that there was someone fool enough to take the lonely, mucky job of dish-washing from them. They thought her mad and kept a respectful distance. Only Carmen, the wide, black and joyous supervisor, recognised that Denise was driven by some urge or other.

'Honey, is you mad or something?' she would ask. 'Why is you always washing?'

'Leave her alone, Mrs Hope,' the others would call, 'she's happy and so's we.'

Carmen would not leave be. 'Why don't you go on the till for a short while? Wash, wash, wash. Take you to church and you would sit in the font.'

Denise would just look up vacantly through the steam that rose sluggishly from a sink of suds and dishes.

Carmen could not understand, but then Carmen, wide and beautiful, was on the side of brightness and of life. A tri-coloured bandana wrapped round her large and handsome head, she filled the greasy kitchen with her idiosyncratic versions of jumbled hymns and pop tunes from the radio.

'Honey,' she would tell Denise in the quieter moments of the day, 'the Lord gives us troubles and he give us something to fight them back and He is joy itself. He is fun and good time. He is a Saturday night and a bottle of sherry with your husband and friends. He is peace and he is a cuddle, too. Do you know of the Lord, Denise? I know you don't for I can tell that way. I can see by your mopy way that you won't recognise Him if He come up and bit your backside off. You the most definitely Lordless thing I seen ever.'

Denise, silently, supposed she was. Being Lordless was getting close to zero, she supposed.

'I prays for you and you not grateful one bit.'

Denise didn't want a prayer. She didn't want her name on anybody's lips whatever.

'Know what?' Carmen would say, cracking an egg and plopping it into a bucket-deep frying pan brimming and snapping with bubbling oil. 'What we all want is fun. A little joy. We all wants that. Why, even an octopus likes to get tickled, you know.'

Denise withdrew even further into herself. What Carmen said was only half the story. Joy had to be paid for, it didn't come free. No, the octopus, after that quick tickle, was grabbed and dunked in boiling water to make a soup out of him. Now, whereas Carmen would have thought the tickle worth the price, Denise felt you need only learn a lesson so many times before it stuck: you snatch joy from misery and what you get is more misery and, knowing what joy is, misery is harder to bear. Think on that, thought Denise, and then you'll love zero like me.

164

As the months passed, Denise communicated less and less and words were replaced by brief nods and curt gestures.

'What words done to you that you don't use them no more?' asked Carmen, strangely hurt.

Carmen and her girls fell in with Denise's ways, but less willingly as time went on. These girls liked laughs, and work was only bearable if it was like a joke shared in good company. Denise really dragged things down.

Carmen did not give up. A supervisor is like a mother to her girls and Denise was one very strange daughter.

'Was it a man made you feel this way?'

Denise flicked back a greasy thread of hair and dunked another trayload of cups into the sink.

'Honey, you just rude. When I says a thing you don't answer me back. You just plain-as-plain-can-be rude.'

Carmen told the girls to leave Denise alone. 'For she is tapped. She is soft in the head and it is probably catching.'

That was how it was. That was how Denise wanted it. That was how she thought it had to be.

No friends. No talking. No nothing. A scruffy nun of a woman.

Chapter Three

The Bolt Hole

When not working she went back home to bombed-out N16.

Home was the top room in a terraced house at the end of a dismal street that stretched for a dismal mile. The house looked empty from the outside. The windows that were not boarded up were hung with sacking, and children had written their names in the thick smears of dust that covered the window on the ground floor. The privet-green paintwork on the door was peeling and the paint on the window-sills had been weathered away. The wood was damp and warped and rotten. Inside, the house was so lousy it could have stood up and walked away. Mice, fat, sleek beasts as tame as pets, moved with smooth assuredness across the dingy hallway with its bleak patchwork of carpet cuttings laid curling end to curling end. Up along the staircase and landings their nests could be found in dark corners. The air was rich with the smell of their droppings. Here, in this house, were the lower depths, and Denise felt lucky to find them.

Apart from the mice the house seemed deserted, but in fact each room was occupied by tenants as shadowy and as seedy as Denise herself. She saw them rarely but heard them often. Somewhere in the house there was a couple who argued relentlessly in a foreign tongue and somewhere else a baby cried continuously, a sickly, mithering howl. There was a man who lived in the next room to her but she never saw him. She knew him for a man by the heaviness of his footsteps as he paced up and down his room and for deep groans he made as he masturbated, his bed thumping against the thin partition wall. The tenants never mingled. The hallway and the stairs were always empty. They took whatever joy there was in a communal life by listening in through cardboard-thin walls on their neighbours' doings. Sounds travelled throughout the house with enormous fidelity, and so it seemed part of the spirit world, haunted by invisible but distinctly audible ghosts. The house knew no landlord and so the noisy ghosts seemed to live there rent-free. No one, it seemed, would admit to owning the ruined house, no one had the nerve to collect rent from its inhabitants or fix the crumbling walls, the rotting banisters or the uncertain plumbing or rid the walls of the intricate road map of damp patches that had traced their way through the peeling anaglypta.

Denise's room was no better. Its floor was covered by a tar-coloured carpet and its walls were covered with a custard-yellow paint that had browned over from age, damp and lack of light. There was a bed, a narrow, lumpy thing, with springs that groaned and snapped at the slightest touch, a table, a hard-backed chair, a Calor gas stove and a sink. She kept her clothes in a black plastic bag and the black dress she'd borrowed from Jacqueline on a nail by the door. A box of paper plates, a cup and a bag of plastic cutlery filched from work stood by her bed, and a clock, the only thing she had kept that had once belonged to Colin. There were no pictures, no ornaments, no fire, no radio, no TV. Books belonged to the days of Colin. It was a room as bare of personality, decoration and life as its occupant.

The place suited Denise. In its dereliction, its ghostliness, its seedy otherness, it was a reflection of her self, her secret motives. It was not a home. It was not a home she wanted. A home is an addition to the self, it comforts and extends it, but as she did not want any self to speak of she certainly did not wish to comfort or extend it. It was a bolt hole where she could escape whoever or whatever it was she feared would divert her from her descent, catch her from her fall. It was a room, a room she went to when she was not working.

When she was there she slept. Work tired her and sleep cut down the amount of living she had to do and when sleep did not come she would sit upright in the hard-backed chair and wait for it, blocking out the noise of the children playing in the street, the foreign squabblings of her neighbours, the bothersome cry of the baby and the bed of the man next door thumping against the wall as he masturbated yet again.

When sleep came she could concentrate once more on the one hard, the one diamond-hard point of her life, on the one thing she knew for certain. Then she could dream of Deborah and how they would one day meet in some shadowy place high up, somewhere well to the left of North.

Chapter Four

Crumbling is Not an Instant Act

The next two significant events in her life were her decision to give up washing herself – it was, after all, lavishing care on an object to which she was indifferent – and losing her job. The two events were connected.

'Honey, you stink and there's no way we's sticking for that too.'

To lose her job was to overcome another barrier in her journey towards zero. Working tied her to the world, forced her to have dealings with others, chained her to the clock. The loss of her job was no big deal, something to celebrate, in fact, except that she did not go in for such things any more.

Now the speed with which she went to seed increased. The steam from the pot-filled sink had made her once dry skin greasy. Blackheads erupted along her nostrils, chin and the curve of her cheek-bone and her poor diet gave her a boil on her neck which she nursed for months. Altogether, her face and her body had the yellow-grey pallor of the unwashed and had become heavy and loose-looking from neglect and fatigue. Her cheeks sank, her lips slackened into an ugly and demanding pout. Her hair was no longer the fiery halo that had caught Colin's attention but a fizzled, dank mophead scraped back into a lank pony tail. It had become a stranger to the comb, and although her body ached and itched for soap and water she was deaf to its demands.

She kept to her room after losing her job. She did not even try to look for another. The dole was enough to keep her. Her ways were simple now and her needs few. She only went out to sign on or cash her giro. She bought the few cans, tea bags and dried milk she needed to feed herself on either one of these journeys. She became well-known at both the dole and the post office. People learnt to stand well away from her, her smell was so offensive. No one offered to help her. No one cared how she was, although she was obviously a wreck. No one seemed to notice her, which was what she wanted.

There is a certain type of beetle which lives in both the country and the town. The beetle is normally the colour of dead leaves, a soft brown. In the city the same beetle would be a deep grey. The colour is protective, camouflage. It allows the beetle to go by unnoticed.

171

Denise, a gnarled, tormented stub of a woman, could walk the streets of N16 unnoticed.

Not that she walked the streets of N16 regularly – Tuesday mornings to sign on and Thursday fortnightly to cash her giro. Otherwise she kept to her room, in which time played elastic tricks and the sounds of the house, its ghostly tenants and busy mice and the fighting of the children in the street outside, made for Denise a cracked and atonal elegy to accompany her vacant hours.

She cleared her mind, emptied it, and thought of nothing. She sat in that chair or lay on that bed where she could hear the mice scratch away at the skirting boards, the mithering cry of the baby. She was a girl with a past, a family, a story to tell, a personality of the dark and passive kind but a personality nevertheless, slowly peeling off each sticky layer of herself, renouncing memory and hope, crumbling. This crumbling was not an instant act but a slow process, willed through determined neglect and indifference.

So she lived on the dole and in that dark room in a silence as painful as it was unbroken. Soon there would be no Denise, only a vacuum, a hole where she had once been. Soon there would be a Deborah to fill that hole.

Deborah.

As a concession to her numb and emptying mind, as a treat when it would no longer lie down and play dead but jump up and beg for attention or exercise from its owner, she would allow herself to imagine Deborah and have conversations with her about the things she saw through the window or complaints about her neighbours.

'The car parked outside is green . . . There's frost on the path this morning . . . I think that foreign couple

172

must be Spanish . . . or Welsh.'

The quality of the conversations was hardly enough to entice a girl back from the dead, but as nothing now happened to her there was little to speak of. She couldn't picture Deborah for long. Sometimes she could call up a hazy, passport photograph of a sullen young woman with a fat face and a perm, but the colour would run and the picture would fade before she could establish it firmly. She could not see her, but she could sense her, feel something like the presence of her in her head, like a draught of warm air inside it.

It did not hurt to try to think of Deborah, although she always drew back from doing so. But what did hurt, what would always hurt, what she could visualise all too easily and too often was that push, that fateful push, the earth collapsing, the bleak Rucks rumbling, Deborah falling, the dust rising in thick, choking clouds.

Nothing could compete with it for pain. When she gave herself up to it this memory could erase everything else. The very walls, those custard-yellow walls, would scatter and the light outside would fail to break through the dirty window pane and she would sit soaked in darkness. Under its immense pressure Denise could sit hour after hour in the hard-backed chair, head flung back so tightly her neck looked as if it had snapped in two, silently but violently screaming Deborah's name, the last, prolonged syllable of which was enough to make her mouth stretch to near tearing point. If the scream had not been silent, if it had been one degree more severe, perhaps it would have ripped her face in two and ended her story, this story, ended it a desert away from where it began, ended it in a zero, well to the left of North.

Chapter Five

A Mystic Shape

One night there was a knock on the door of her room. It was what she had been waiting for with a mixture of dread and delight, but now that it had come dread seemed to drown delight.

She had been asleep, stretched out on top of the bed, still clothed. The second she heard it she sat up bolt upright and ran to the door to answer it. But when she reached the door the question of who it could be acted like clamps on her legs. She stopped, restrained by that question.

The room was quite in darkness, just a fraction of

evening light left for her to see the dim outlines of the room and the soft fog the cold air made of her breath. She put her ear to the crack of the door and her hand wavered around its handle. She could hear nothing, only the sound of her own breathing and the crack of the floorboards beneath her.

The knock came again, a succession of three knocks, quick, loud, rapping. Denise jerked back as if the blows on the door had been meant for her. Yet still, the knocking apart, there was no sound from beyond the door.

She crouched down and tried to see if there was anybody there, but the landing light had been turned off or was broken again and she could see nothing. Dreading that the knocks might come again, for she knew whatever it was it meant her damage, she opened the door slowly. She peered out into the dark landing. Nothing. Nobody. Braver still, she came out and stood awhile, listening. The baby whimpered, a burst of laughter came from behind a door somewhere downstairs, a mouse walked past, its claws making a slow and regular scratching noise on the linoleum. She knew those sounds. She was not moved to fear by them for, eery though they were, she was familiar with them, but there was, and this is hard to explain, a noise that could not be heard somewhere in that house, somewhere close by, a silence where a noise should be, the soft noise of someone standing close by her, by her door, ready to knock again.

Denise, detecting this silence, guessing at its particular shape, withdrew to her room, closing the door quietly, the barest click, and returned to her chair with her hands folded in her lap to prevent them from shaking.

She knew what the knocks meant. Deborah was

coming out of her head. She was returning to the world and wasn't this what Denise had been waiting for, preparing for? Now that it was coming true she was no longer sure and she became scared for the life she had considered so unimportant, scared that Deborah would take it from her. The knocks on the door were only the start of it. Deborah was playing cat to Denise's mouse.

What happened next was the waiting. The waiting lasted a long time – a week, a month, a year, a day. Time had grown elastic. It stretched and contracted at will. Time had grown blank and had lost its markings. Time took a long time to be time. Time was as long as a piece of string.

Waiting had been what she had been doing since Colin, since before Colin, since Deborah, but this waiting had a different quality. It was sharper, tenser. This was a waiting with a point to it, with an end to it. She was waiting for that knock to come again and this time she would be braver. There would be no hesitation. She would open the door the second it came, but it did not come again and so she waited.

Instead, one night, the phone downstairs in the hall rang, the phone which did not work rang. It rang once, twice, again, again. No one answered it. Denise didn't. She was waiting for the knock.

When the phone rang again the next night, or was it the same night, it did not stop. Denise pulled the blanket from off the bed around her shoulders and padded down to the hallway. She switched on the light. The naked bulb swang in the draught from the broken letter-box and two flies drew perfect circles around it. She came to the phone and as she reached out her hand to pick it up the ringing stopped. She scampered back to her room in case she was seen.

It rang again the next night and the next. It rang and it rang and the ringing always stopped just as she reached out to pick up the receiver.

No one hears this but me, she thought. When it happens it is the only sound in the house, in the whole world. It's for me, this ringing, for me alone.

One night she anticipated. She sat at the bottom of the stairs, the dark hallway lit only by the orange lamplight that slipped through the letter-box. It did not ring that night.

She gave up. She simply turned over in her bed when she heard it again, twisting the grimy sheets tight round herself, her face to the wall, head buried under her pillow to muffle the sound of the phone.

On and on it rang, louder and more persistent until it seemed to be sitting inside her skull, rasping away, filing down her lobes until she could stand it no more and, struggling from her sheets, she ran down the stairs and grabbed at the phone, screaming into it.

'I'm here, I'm here. I'm waiting. Why don't you come? Can you hear me? Why don't you come? I'm waiting. Can you hear me? Can you?'

She filled her mouth with saliva, spat into the phone and crashed it down. She fell back against the banister and sank down the cold, damp wall, sobbing. She could stand no more, no more. Now, she decided, she would scream a scream so loud and high her voice would crack and the house would splinter apart.

Deborah!

No one heard. No one came. Perhaps, like the phone,

the scream could only be heard by her.

No matter, the screaming of that name brought Denise peace. Deborah had heard her. Deborah was here. She could feel that she was no longer alone. How stupid to think she had ever been entirely alone. There had always been Deborah. Best friend Deborah. Deborah, giving her comfort and company in the cold hallway in the dead of night. She could feel her breath, warm on her cheek. She was aware of how a mystic shape moved behind her and drew her head back by the hair.

'Hello, Deborah,' she said and waited for a reply.

None came.

Not yet.

Chapter Six

Deborah

She saw Deborah the next day on the way to the dole.

A plump blonde woman in a yellow overcoat and red boots waved at Denise from the other side of the road. She pointed to the door of the pub behind her, gestured that she was going in there for a drink and did Denise want to join her. She shouted something but the traffic was so loud that Denise could not hear her. The woman laughed, pushing back her round fair head as she did so, then turned and went into the pub, beckoning Denise.

'That's Deborah,' she murmured incredulously. 'That's Deborah.'

She was shocked and disappointed. She had expected a column of light to fall from the sky and the earth to sing at Deborah's resurrection, and Deborah herself was to be golden and glowing, not a fat blonde in a yellow mackintosh. Have I been through all this to be rewarded by that? Yet it was indisputably Deborah. A plump blonde girl grown into a plump blonde woman. And now here she was, across the road, in that pub, waiting for Denise to join her.

She shivered, paused before stepping off the kerb, uncertain as to what to do and suddenly unwilling. Once off the kerb and the first step taken, the next came automatically. It took only a few more to cross the road and enter the pub.

It was a grave of a pub, dark, cold, smelling of beer and lemon polish and empty but for an old woman, mean and sharp-faced, in a red paisley blouse, blue-grey hair piled high like a marble turret. This was not Deborah but there was no one else there.

'We're closed,' the woman snapped at the blank-faced tramp who had just walked in.

'I'm looking for someone.' Her voice was shaky from disuse. 'Have you seen no one come in?'

'No, I haven't. We're open in ten minutes. Now, outside.'

Denise tugged at a greasy strand of hair, uncertain of what to do.

'Frank!' The marble turret of hair quivered dangerously as she called the name.

Frank, beer belly first, came through the swing doors of the lounge bar in answer to the landlady's cry.

'Frank,' she repeated, nodding at Denise. 'Get her out of here. Dirty tramp.'

Frank lumbered over to Denise and took her gently by the arm.

'No, let us stay here for a minute. Please, I've not been well, you see.'

'No way, dearie.' His beery breath fell over her in thick waves, making her feel faint. She had not eaten in days. 'Back home with you. Home's the best place for you.'

'I aint got no home,' she said icily, aiming for dignity. 'I only came in here to see if a friend were here but she weren't. I were mistaken. I think I will leave by myself now.'

She sailed out of the door and back onto the street. She stood hesitantly on the kerb, looking as if she were unsure how to cross the road.

A mistake had been made. That was all. She had anticipated. She had been too eager and had broken the rules. It was another of Deborah's games, like the knocks on the door, the ringing of the telephone. But each time Deborah came a little nearer. Deborah would meet her soon. She would stop this teasing game of hide and seek and appear out in the open. She would touch her arm in the street and say, 'Hallo, remember me?', and it would be Deborah. It would be a full-grown Deborah and Deborah would be all forgiveness. Denise smiled, imagining that mercy, which would be as warming as the hot soapy baths she now denied herself. They would laugh and fall into each other's arms. Deborah, a full-grown woman, fair and pretty and always laughing, not a fat blonde in a yellow mackintosh or a corpse covered in blood and slack at the bottom of a muddy mineshaft.

'Denise,' she would say, 'Denise Monton?'

'Deborah?'

'Den.'

'Deb.'

'It's good to see you.'

'And you, Deb, and you.'

'Like a drink, Den?'

They would sit in a pub all evening and they'd gossip, exchange news, catch up on each other's histories. Denise would tell her about Colin and Deborah would laugh and say, 'Men!'

'You were always my best friend, Deborah.'

'Your bestest friend?'

'My very bestest.'

They'd take a walk together, arm in arm.

'We'll meet often now.'

'We should never have lost touch.'

'My fault, Deborah, my fault.'

'Nobody's fault, Denise. It's all gone, all past.'

'We're friends.'

'Firm friends.'

'We can take a flat. Share one.'

'Or a house. Just us two.'

'A house. In Little Atherton?'

'Why not? Yes. On the Rucks.'

'Yeah, right on top of them. We'll build one.'

'And live there.'

'Just you and me.'

'With the Rucks as our back garden.'

'Lovely.'

'Lovely.'

No, that would not do. That would not do at all. That was day-dreaming, that was anticipating. What would happen would happen as Deborah wished it. She'd no business anticipating it.

It was not Denise's business to anticipate. The future

was not hers to imagine or dictate. Her business was to travel on, pulling and tugging the heavy cart she had elected for herself through the dark. A tired, clapped-out pit pony of a woman, too long in the dark to look on the gift of light as anything but the bringer of blindness.

She finally stepped off the kerb. She did not look for or even consider the traffic. If Deborah wanted her dead under the wheels of a truck, then Deborah would make sure the truck would find Denise. There was no doubt about that. There was no doubt that Deborah could be trusted, could be relied upon.

Abacus now offers an exciting range of quality titles by both established and new authors. All of the books in this series are available from:
  Sphere Books,
  Cash Sales Department,
  P.O. Box 11,
  Falmouth,
  Cornwall TR10 9EN.

Alternatively you may fax your order to the above address. Fax No. 0326 76423.

Payments can be made as follows: Cheque, postal order (payable to Macdonald & Co (Publishers) Ltd) or by credit cards, Visa/Access. Do not send cash or currency. UK customers: please send a cheque or postal order (no currency) and allow 80p for postage and packing for the first book plus 20p for each additional book up to a maximum charge of £2.00.

B.F.P.O. customers please allow 80p for the first book plus 20p for each additional book.

Overseas customers including Ireland, please allow £1.50 for postage and packing for the first book, £1.00 for the second book, and 30p for each additional book.

NAME (Block Letters) ....

ADDRESS ....

....

☐ I enclose my remittance for _____

☐ I wish to pay by Access/Visa Card

Number ☐☐☐☐☐☐☐☐☐☐☐☐☐☐☐☐☐☐☐

Card Expiry Date ☐☐☐☐